THE VOYAGE OF THE JAVELIN

The Black Buccaneer
Down the Big River
Longshanks
Red Horse Hill
Away to Sea
King of the Hills
Lumberjack
The Will to Win and Other Stories
Who Rides in the Dark?
T-Model Tommy
Bat: The Story of a Bull Terrier
Boy with a Pack
Clear for Action!
Blueberry Mountain
Shadow in the Pines
The Sea Snake
The Long Trains Roll
Skippy's Family
Jonathan Goes West
Behind the Ranges
River of the Wolves
Cedar's Boy
Whaler 'Round the Horn
Bulldozer
The Fish Hawk's Nest
Sparkplug of the Hornets
The Buckboard Stranger
Guns for the Saratoga
Sabre Pilot
Everglades Adventure
The Commodore's Cup

The Voyage of the Javelin

STEPHEN W. MEADER

Illustrated by John O'Hara Cosgrave II

HARCOURT, BRACE AND COMPANY, NEW YORK

THE VOYAGE OF THE JAVELIN

FOREWORD

The Age of the Clipper Ship—surely the greatest era in the history of merchant sail—lasted only about twenty-six years. Few of us today realize how brief was the glory of the great Yankee square-riggers that carried the flag so proudly to all the ports of the world.

During that quarter century more than two hundred of the swift and graceful ships were launched from American yards all the way from Maine to the Carolinas. Their builders, their captains, and, above all, the vessels themselves bore names famous around the globe. Everyone knew of the speedy voyages of such ships as *Oriental, Game-Cock, Surprise, Challenge, Flying Cloud, Young America, Stag Hound,* and *Sovereign of the Seas.* Everyone had heard of the men like Donald McKay, William Webb, and Samuel Hall who built them; and of their captains—Palmer, Dumaresq, Creesy, and Waterman among a hundred others.

Forerunners of the true clipper ships were swift-sailing privateers built in Baltimore during the War of 1812. They had the slim lines and raked masts that would later be incorporated in bigger ships for the China and California trade. In the middle 1840's, while the British were still depending on broad-beamed, lumbering vessels to bring tea and spices from the East, the Yankee builders came up with a design that could literally sail circles around them. The British Navigation Act had allowed no commerce to England except in British ships. But the repeal of the act, in 1849, opened the door to other nations, and it was these

7

fast American skysail-yarders that ran off with the profitable tea trade.

The greatest impetus to clipper building, however, came with the discovery of gold in California. Fortunes were made overnight in ships that sailed around the Horn to San Francisco, and the 1850's saw the full flowering of the Age of Sail.

The end came with surprising suddenness. Three things doomed the clippers. First was the War Between the States. Confederate raiders sank or captured merchant vessels by the score in both Atlantic and Pacific and made California voyages far too hazardous. Second was the rapid development of steam engines and boilers for marine use. And the final blow was the opening of the Suez Canal in 1869. Since only steam vessels could navigate the canal, sailing ships were practically eliminated from the China and East India trade.

For this book I have chosen a period at the high tide of the clipper era. Many of the ships and people mentioned are real, and the fictitious ones are as true to type as I can make them. The *Javelin,* as well as the boys who went to sea in her, is in the latter group.

For those who may worry about what might have happened to Bob Wingate and Matt Ryder when sail gave way to steam, I can offer some reassurance. Both of them would probably have earned masters' certificates when the Civil War began. Both would have served with honor in the Navy. And in later years Bob would in all likelihood have captained an ocean liner, while Matt settled down to being a Boston merchant.

S. W. M.

I

For weeks Bob Wingate had been looking forward to the Fourth of July. Not just because he could join in the usual celebration—the parades and bonfires and the noise of bells, horns, and firecrackers. He had done that plenty of times. But this July 4 would be *launching day!*

To almost any boy who lived along the New England coast that summer of 1854, the launching of a new clipper ship was an event far bigger than any mere fireworks display. Not even a circus could rival it in excitement.

Bob had a special interest in the great wooden hull that stood on the ways in Portsmouth. He lived only a few miles away, in the town of Kittery, Maine, just across the Narrows. And he had actually helped make some of the cordage for the ship, working in his father's ropewalk. Every time he was in Portsmouth, he made a beeline for the Rogers and Hale yard, back on the harborfront. There he saw her grow, from the laying of the keel and the setting of the great oak ribs to the final planking of her hull.

Some of the workmen knew him and would let him hold a hank of oakum while they calked her seams, or even drive a copper nail or two. Often he would stand and stare upward at her long and lovely lines, the sharp, slim flare of her bows. He thought then she was the most beautiful thing created by the hands of men.

Her name was the *Javelin,* and she was being built for Eli Chase, the famous Boston shipowner. She was 200 feet long, with a beam of 39 feet, and her register would be 1,460 tons—not the biggest clipper ever built in the Portsmouth yards, but a size that many captains considered best for speed and handling at sea. She was larger than the *Red Rover,* for instance, but smaller than the *Typhoon.*

There was one feature of this launching that set it apart from all the others Bob had witnessed. The *Javelin* would be sent down the ways with masts and standing rigging already in place! Old salts and dockside loafers held divided opinions about the attempt. Some said that Old Man Rogers knew what he was about and all would go off smoothly. Others insisted the top-heavy craft would capsize before ever she hit the water. In any case, all of Portsmouth and the surrounding countryside meant to be on hand to see what happened.

Bob had turned sixteen that spring. He was a big, freckle-faced youngster, close to six feet tall, and weighed 165 stripped. Looking him over, his father had decided that he was now a man, and it was time for him to leave the academy and start to do a man's work. That, of course, meant making rope. Bob, on the other hand, wanted above all else to go to sea. He had tried to argue the point with his father but made little progress. A parent's word was law in those days, and Tobias Wingate ruled that the proper place for him was in the ropeworks, not before the mast.

"A sailor's life," he told his son sternly, "isn't fit for a dog. I sailed a couple o' voyages to the West Indies when I was young, an' I know. You're in rough, Godless company. You risk your life a dozen times a day, an' the pay's less'n half what you can make ashore."

Sailing on a coasting schooner with salt fish or lumber for Jamaica, Bob could have pointed out, was quite different from a clipper voyage to California. But he kept his mouth shut and did as he was told. When school ended in June, he began work in the long shed, known as the ropewalk, where he twisted strong yellow fibers of Manila hemp into strands, and the strands into rope. The machines were crude affairs, and there was a lot of pulling and walking. It was a tedious job, but fine for developing arm, wrist, and leg muscles.

Meanwhile, at every chance he got, the boy went out in his fourteen-foot dory. He had a small line of lobster pots that he tended each evening, keeping the family supplied and selling the balance of his catch to the local storekeeper. Good as they tasted, lobsters weren't worth much—only ten cents apiece for good-sized ones—but it gave him a little spending money over and above his seventy-five cents a day in wages.

When the breeze was right, he hoisted the little triangular sail and cruised luxuriously up the Piscataqua River and sometimes as far as Great Bay. The Narrows themselves were tricky, for the tide ran through like a millrace, and a contrary wind could kick up choppy seas. Bob had to learn a lot about tides and currents to navigate that stretch of water safely.

*　　*　　*

At midnight, the night before the Fourth, the bell in the Kittery Congregational Church began to ring with a deafening clangor. Bob woke up at once and put on his clothes. A glance out the window told him it was a fine, starlit night, with the promise of a fair day to follow.

He tiptoed out of the house and went to the woodshed, where there were two homemade torches he had prepared for the occasion. They were simply poles, five or six feet long, with rags tied to their tops, soaked in kitchen grease. He felt in his pocket to make sure he had matches, took the torches, and hurried toward the little square, where he knew the parade would be assembling.

As he approached, a drum began to beat, and two cornets

and a trombone, inexpertly played, burst into a ragged march tune. It was a minute or more before he realized they were playing "Yankee Doodle."

Nearly a hundred boys and men were gathering in the square. Bob found several of his former schoolmates and joined them as the line began to form.

"Hey, Wingate," one called to him. "You got any matches? I clean forgot mine."

He lighted the first of his own torches and held the flickering flame to the one held by the other boy. Then he fell into step behind the musicians. They marched all the way to the ferry slip, turned, and countermarched through the town, whooping, cheering, and making as much noise as possible. Lamps and candles were lighted in the houses along the route. Like it or not, Kittery was awake.

As more and more people came out to watch, the marchers led the way to the pile of old barrels and scrap lumber in Nelsons' pasture. The ranks broke and one boy after another ran to set a corner of the pile ablaze with his torch. Within seconds the flames were roaring upward. Fifty feet high they sprang into the air. They reddened half the sky, and one man said afterward he had light enough to read a newspaper a mile from the scene.

By two-thirty the flames were dying down and the noise subsiding into a widely scattered snap of firecrackers. Bob went home and crawled into bed once more. He could still get a few hours of sleep before breakfast time.

Broad daylight roused him at six-thirty, and already it gave promise of being a hot day. The wind was westerly, off the land. Bob pulled on a clean shirt and a pair of dungarees and went downstairs to breakfast. Because of the holiday nobody was expected to work at the ropewalk.

"You going over to the launching?" his mother asked. "Better dress up a little before you leave."

Bob laughed. "Everybody's going to be looking at the ship, Ma, not at me," he replied. "Besides, it's too hot for a Sunday coat, an' I'm going to row across. Want me to take you?"

"No, thanks," she said. "There's a morning's work to do. Your father and I'll take the ferry. Don't get yourself into any scrapes over there, now."

He promised lightheartedly and set about making himself a couple of sandwiches. The launching had been set for noon, but it might be later, and he knew he would be hungry.

The rickety dock where he kept his dory tied stood high out of water, its piling green-scummed and crusted with barnacles. The tide was past the ebb and beginning to flood. With a west wind blowing, the Narrows would be choppy. He cast off the painter, jumped aboard, and dropped the oars in the deep-worn chocks.

Having been in and around boats all his life, Bob was a stout rower. Still he was wet with sweat and spray before he had pulled half the distance to Portsmouth. The tide carried him sidewise, and the crosswind tossed wave crests over the gunwale. At last he got over into the lee of the New Hampshire shore and let the current carry him on around the point. From there he got his first full view of the ship.

She stood high above the sheds and cranes and warehouses, her rigging brave with flags that whipped in the breeze. Her long hull was painted a glistening black, and below the water line she gleamed with bright copper. The great masts and topmasts, with the pronounced rake aft that was a clipper ship trademark, shone with varnish. The mainmast, he had been told, was a "King's pine," marked a hundred years before with the royal broad arrow. It was a solid forty-eight inches through at the butt and ran straight and true all the way to the crosstrees without a single knot. The topgallant masts would not be sent up until her rigging was completed after the launching.

Workmen still swarmed on the *Javelin*'s deck, putting last-minute touches to her gear. As soon as Bob had tied up his dory, he hurried over to the ways. Abijah Lowe, the foreman of the yard, was a Kittery man and recognized the freckle-faced boy as a neighbor.

"Well, young Wingate," he said heartily, "goin' to be on hand to see her go, are ye?"

Bob grinned. "Didn't think you could keep me away, did you? Everything ready for it? I suppose you'll wait for high tide."

"That an' the visitors," said Lowe. "We've got the owners comin', an' folks from Boston an' Salem an' all over. Can't start till they're on hand. Hey, you, Sandy—coil down that loose line!"

Bob walked along beside the shoring timbers that held the hull in place. When he reached the bow and looked upward, he saw that the figurehead had been put on since his last visit. It was finely carved to represent a Greek warrior, helmeted and holding a shield and a short spear. The carving, life-size, gleamed with a freshly applied coat of gold leaf. It was the finishing touch to the beauty of the ship. Just to look at it brought a catch in the boy's throat.

By eleven o'clock the townspeople were beginning to gather. Some brought campstools or baskets to sit on and picked out strategic places on the steep slope overlooking the yard. Nearly all had picnic lunches, and soon they were gnawing at fried chicken or munching sandwiches. Bob got out his own food and ate it while he watched the throng increase. His father and mother didn't appear until after the bell in the nearby church had struck twelve. The ferry must have been overloaded and running late. However, he saw them find vantage points high up at the rear of the crowd.

At twelve-thirty a band began playing, and shortly after that Bob saw a procession of carriages approaching. The tide was just about full. If these newcomers were the important guests, it looked as if the launching could soon take place.

The first carriage, an open barouche drawn by a pair of handsome blacks and driven by a liveried coachman, was a familiar sight around Portsmouth. It belonged to Mr. Hale, banker and shipbuilder, reputed to be one of the richest men in town. Next came Mr. Rogers' carriage, and three others followed, containing the mayor and other city dignitaries.

Bob watched the people get out. The gentlemen were elegant enough in top hats, tail coats, and fawn-colored trousers, but it was the ladies who attracted most attention. Their modish gowns were of rustling silk and satin, and their hats were so covered with flowers that they looked like miniature gardens.

With Mrs. Hale was an extraordinarily pretty woman, not young but beautifully dressed, her brown hair in a mass of ringlets at the back of her head. She carried a yellow parasol and had a funny-looking little pug dog at the end of a leash. Bob had seen only one pug before, but he knew they came from China. Putting two and two together, he was fairly certain the lady must be Mrs. Chase, wife of the great Boston shipowner. As everybody knew, Eli Chase had made a fortune in the China trade long before the California gold rush started. The *Javelin* was to be the newest ship in the Chase fleet.

While the guests chatted, Bob sat down on the end of a stringer and finished his sandwiches. Then Mr. Hale stood up on the flag-decorated platform and made a speech of

welcome to Mr. and Mrs. Chase and the friends they had brought from Boston. After that it was Eli Chase's turn. He complimented the shipwrights of Portsmouth and mentioned some of the famous clippers they had built, carrying the stars and stripes to every port in the world. At last he came to the purpose for which they were gathered on this anniversary of American independence—to launch a new queen of the seas.

Loud applause greeted his remarks, and there was a stir-

ring in the crowd as people sought better positions from which to watch.

The christening of a ship was done without much formality in those days. As a rule, the builder or the yard foreman smashed a bottle of ordinary rum on the vessel's stem, yelled out her name, and gave the signal that sent her down the ways. This time it was to be done more elaborately.

A staging had been erected just below the figurehead on the sharp prow. Bob saw Mrs. Chase climb this scaffold with a beribboned champagne bottle in her daintily gloved hand. Meanwhile, the workmen hurried to the ways carrying slush pots full of grease, and other men stood by the shoring timbers, with mauls in their fists, ready to knock out the props at the foreman's command.

Bob was standing down near the vessel's stern, a few yards from the water that now lapped the ways. He could see that Abijah Lowe was flustered. The man's face was red and streaming with perspiration as his big moment drew near. Mrs. Chase was in position on the staging now, standing beside her husband.

"Ready?" she called out, laughing and excited. "I christen thee"—and she swung the bottle crashing against the bow—"*Javelin!*"

At the same instant Abijah Lowe roared "Let her go!" and the shoring timbers toppled, the hull began to slide down the greased ways. The crowd watched, silent and expectant. Then suddenly Bob heard a high-pitched scream.

"Ling Foo!" Mrs. Chase cried. "Oh—he'll be killed!"

The boy saw a tawny streak flash by and heard a bark. The pug, dragging its leash, was racing toward the slippery timbers of the ways, where the ship was already gathering momentum. Bob didn't stop to think. He made a dive for the end of the trailing leash and jerked the little dog back just as the hull slid past.

II

For a moment Bob lay there panting. When he got to his feet, still holding a firm grip on the leather thong, the *Javelin* had roared into the water. A huge white wave from her stern was lashing out across the river. But she floated upright, tall and stately like the queen she was.

The pug, furiously excited, turned on its rescuer now and grabbed a fold of Bob's dungarees in its teeth. Bob got to one knee, patted the little brute's side, and spoke reassuringly till the dog let go its hold. By that time there seemed to be a lot of people around him. He looked up to see Abijah Lowe and the great shipowner, Eli Chase, himself.

Chase smiled and took the leash in one hand. He held out the other hand to Bob.

"My lad," he said with feeling, "you've done us a real service. This launching day might have turned out sadly for my wife. She sets great store by little Ling Foo, here. I trust his teeth didn't break the skin when he nipped you."

Bob pulled up his trouser leg above the calf. There were no marks on the flesh, and in fact the tough dungaree cloth was hardly torn. The boy grinned.

"No harm done at all, sir," he replied. "I guess the dog's just not used to launchings."

"Come with me," Chase told him. "My wife will want to thank you, I know."

When they reached the little group by the flag-decked platform, the other ladies were still fluttering about Mrs.

Chase, offering her handkerchiefs and smelling salts. But she was over her fright now.

Moist-eyed but smiling, she held out both hands to Bob. "That was a brave thing you did!" she exclaimed. "And you were so quick! I don't know how we can ever make it up to you."

Then she reached out her arms for the funny-faced little pug, scolding it and cooing baby talk at it by turns till Bob fairly squirmed to hear her. Fortunately, he didn't have to listen long. Mr. Hale and Mr. Rogers came to shake his hand. He could see that both were immensely relieved. They must have been upset when tragedy threatened to mar the launching of their clipper.

Standing just behind them was another gentleman Bob hadn't seen before. He was a big square figure in a blue coat. Under craggy gray brows his eyes were direct and piercing, with crow's-feet at their corners. Now he stepped forward with a roll in his gait that made it obvious he was a seafaring man.

Abijah Lowe must have given Chase Bob's name, for the shipowner laid a hand on his shoulder and introduced him.

"Bob Wingate," he said, "this is Captain Jonathan Sprague, who will be in command of the *Javelin*. I think he'd like a word with you."

The captain took Bob's hand in a mighty grip. "I saw you pull that dog out o' trouble," he said gruffly. "Showed some presence o' mind. Ever been to sea?"

"No, sir," the boy answered. "It's what I've always wanted to do, though."

"This your home port?"

"Near enough. I live over across the river—in Kittery."

The captain nodded. "Wingate, eh? I've used Wingate cordage. Any relation?"

"My father owns the ropeworks—yes, sir. He wants me to work there, now school's over."

"But you'd rather go to sea?" asked Captain Sprague with a twinkle in his eye. "Maybe I'd better have a talk with him."

Bob's heart leaped. This conversation all seemed to be pointing in one direction, but he hardly dared believe it meant what he thought.

"My dad," he said in a half-choked voice, "ought to be right up there in the crowd. Want me to try an' find him?"

"I'll go with you," the captain replied with a smile.

The spectators who had packed the slope overlooking the shipyard were beginning to straggle off now that the great event was over. Bob spied his father and mother just as they were leaving and hurried after them.

"Dad," he panted, "there's somebody here wants to speak to you. It's Captain Jonathan Sprague—the skipper of the *Tornado* when she beat the *Wildfire* to San Francisco last year."

His father frowned. "Cap'n Sprague?" he asked. "Wants to see *me?* Don't tell me some of our rope's shown up bad aboard his ship!"

"It isn't that," said Bob. "Here he is—he'll tell you himself. Captain Sprague, this is Tobias Wingate, my father."

Mrs. Wingate, too, was introduced, and the famous clipper master put the couple at ease at once.

"Fine boy you've got," he told them. "Don't know whether you could see what he did from up here, but it was a nice seamanlike job. That dog o' Mrs. Chase's slipped his cable an' he'd have been a goner if young Bob hadn't brought him up all standing. Mr. Chase is mighty grateful. He'd like to reward the lad some way, an' he's offered to let him sail in the *Javelin* if I'm agreeable—which I am. Not as just another seaman, mind you. He'd go as ship's boy, training for an officer's berth. We think he's the right kind o' material. What do you say to that?"

Taken off his guard, Tobias Wingate was hardly prepared to argue, and the burly captain had had a chance to state his case without interruption. Now he saw the dubious look on the ropemaker's face.

"Think it over," he said. "I can't stop to talk any longer. I'm due at the Wentworth House for the dinner they're giving. But just remember—a chance like this doesn't come along every day. I'll be here this week an' next, getting the ship ready to tow to Boston. Let me know when you've made up your mind."

He bowed to Mrs. Wingate. "Your servant, Ma'am," he said, and turned to rejoin the party by the carriages.

Much as Bob wanted to plead with his father, he had sense enough to keep his mouth shut for the moment.

"I've got the dory down there," he said at last. "Want me to row you home?"

Tobias Wingate shook his head. "Thanks," he said, "but we'll take the ferry. Your mother an' I need time to think an' talk this over."

Bob left them and went down past the empty ways, where a few workmen were carrying away timbers and picking up tools. One or two of them looked after him enviously, for the word of Mr. Chase's offer had spread through the yard grapevine. But Bob was unaware of the attention he attracted. With his head in the clouds he stumbled down to the dory, cast off the painter, and shoved off. Out there in the river lay the great sleek hull of the *Javelin,* anchored now. He rowed out and circled the ship once before starting for the Narrows.

"Dear Lord," he prayed under his breath, "make Dad willing to let me go."

When he swung the bow eastward, he saw a little side-wheel steamboat puffing across the channel. It was the ferry. If his parents had caught it, they would be home ahead of him. He let the outrunning tide carry him down the river and rowed in to his own dock. From there he could just make out the upper spars of the clipper, swinging at her moorings. He could hardly bear to take his eyes off her, but finally he turned and walked slowly up the path toward home. There was only one reason why he dawdled. He was afraid of what his father's verdict might be.

The house seemed strangely quiet, and he thought for a moment that his parents must have missed the ferry. Then he heard low voices in the front room. Tiptoeing across the kitchen, barefooted, he reached the door in time to hear his mother speaking.

"Of course we'll miss him, Tobias," she said. "But he's almost a man grown now, and he'd leave us sooner or later. You know the boy's got the sea in his blood. You'll be proud of him some day when he comes home from China, master of his own ship."

Bob heard his father take a deep breath. "All right, Martha," he said at last. "I won't stand in his way, much as I'd hoped to keep him with me in the ropemaking. Cap'n Sprague's a fine man, well spoken of everywhere. I reckon we ought to be glad Bob's sailing under him an' not just shipping out before the mast."

The boy's first impulse was to rush in and hug them both. Instead, he stole back as he had come, slammed the screen door, and sang out a "hello" as if he had just entered.

"We're in here, Robert," his mother called. "Come in— if you're sure your feet are clean."

That last phrase was so familiar the boy couldn't help laughing out loud. He wiped his bare soles on the hooked rug in the kitchen and went to the parlor door, trying to look innocent of any knowledge. His father frowned and cleared his throat.

"Well, son," he said, "we've sort o' decided to take Mr. Chase up on his offer. If you don't mind making another trip across, I reckon we ought to go an' tell him an' Cap'n Sprague so before the party leaves for Boston."

Bob grinned. "Dad," he replied, "I guess you know how I feel. I'd row all the way from here to Cape Ann on that kind of an errand!"

At his mother's urging he put on shoes and a light jacket and changed his dungarees for a pair of clean trousers. They reached Portsmouth about three o'clock and walked up the hill to the hotel, where the diners were still at table.

"Don't want to go barging in on 'em," Tobias Wingate said. "Let's sit out here on the porch till they're through eating."

That was where they were when the party broke up a few minutes later. They heard the ladies withdraw to one of the parlors and caught a whiff of cigar smoke that told them the men were now relaxing over their wine. Bob's father led the way toward the dining room. As they reached the door, Eli Chase saw them and rose with a smile.

"Come in, gentlemen," he said. "I trust your news is good."

Bob had been feeling nine feet tall ever since his father had reached his decision. Now, in the presence of all these celebrities, he almost wished he could crawl under the table. Tobias Wingate, fortunately, was not embarrassed. He shook Chase's hand warmly, thanked him for his kindness, and expressed his pleasure that Bob would be sailing under as fine a skipper as Captain Sprague.

The captain himself took the boy aside. "Glad it turned out so," he said. "We'll sign you on next week an' you can make the trip to Boston. Won't hurt to get a bit o' seamanship pounded into you before we really start to sea. I don't think you expect any favors an' you won't get 'em. You'll be subject to the ship's discipline like all the rest o' the crew, so get your gear together an' report to me at the yard on Monday."

* * *

24

For the next few days Bob thought of little besides his coming apprenticeship in the *Javelin*. He signed the ship's papers on Monday, joining the skeleton crew of sailors and ship fitters who would make her ready for sea. He might have slept on shore, as some of the local men did, but preferred to bunk in the roomy forecastle. As in most of the California clippers, the crew's quarters had been moved topside from the dark and crowded space under the foredeck to a comfortable superstructure just abaft the foremast.

The galley was operating, even though there was no regular cook aboard. The men made shift to get their own meals, and they stood watches much as if they were at sea. Meanwhile, the work of rigging, scouring, and painting went on steadily. The steam tug *R. B. Forbes* was due in the harbor July 15, and Captain Sprague meant to have his ship ready by then to leave for Boston.

Only one of the mates was aboard—the third officer—a young man from Belfast, Maine, by the name of Rodney Snow. He had started as a ship's boy three years before, just as Bob was starting now. In addition, there were the regular ship's carpenter, whose real name was Johnson but who was always known as "Chips," and the bosun, a rough and ready sailor called Red Gilman.

It was just as well that Bob had been warned to expect no favors. Gilman took him in hand from the moment he was signed on and treated him as he would any other raw landlubber. Bob learned fast. He had worked around cordage long enough to know the names and uses of many of the ropes, but plenty of other things were new to him. Most of his first day was spent holystoning the deck. The fact that the planking was brand new made no difference, for holystoning would help to even it and get rid of splinters.

Bob's back was one big ache by the time he was allowed

to knock off for supper. However, he told himself, nobody got to be a real sailor without going through some painful experiences, and his determination to become one was as strong as ever. He was in pretty good physical condition to start with, and the work he did—pulling, lifting, climbing, and swabbing—hardened him up fast.

By the end of that first week he could swarm up the ratlines almost as fast as an able seaman. And at the bosun's shouted order he could lay his hand on the right rope and start hauling. It was a lot easier, he realized, with the ship lying in harbor than it would be at sea in a gale. But at least he was making a beginning.

Meanwhile, the fitters and riggers made good time at their jobs. The weather stayed hot and dry, with only one or two brief thundershowers to interrupt the work. Ten days after the launching the topgallant masts were in place, and the yards were swung up, one after another. The main yard was a monstrous thing, two feet thick and more than ninety feet long, and the rest were in proportion. It took stout tackle to hoist and handle such spars, and it would take a stout crew to man the halyards and braces at sea.

Captain Sprague came aboard every day to check up on the riggers and urge them to greater speed. Occasionally, he would shout an order from the quarterdeck, where he had a view of the whole ship forward. He never appeared to notice Bob but once. That was to upbraid him for resting when he should have been swabbing the deck. The boy didn't feel any resentment, for such reprimands were handed out impartially to everybody aboard, including the young third mate.

By sundown on the fourteenth the captain appeared to be satisfied at last. The *Javelin* was ready to start for Boston on schedule.

Bob stood his watch as usual that night. Harbor watches were easy, and he had ample time to look up at the stars.

wheeling slowly across the sky. He knew the names of most of the constellations. What would it be like, he wondered, to sail in southern seas, where the big dipper and his other friends were no longer visible? In a few months he would find out.

III

He was asleep in his bunk next morning when the *R. B. Forbes* came steaming in around New Castle Point. It was a blast from the tug's whistle that woke him. He hurried out on deck and saw her coming up the Narrows, her paddle wheels slapping in the choppy tide.

Now that the time for departure was coming close, Bob had a sudden qualm of homesickness. He asked the mate for permission to go ashore long enough to see his parents, and Snow granted it, warning him to be back aboard by ten o'clock.

Bob didn't wait for breakfast but got into the first boat going to Portsmouth and caught the ferry at six-thirty. He hurried up to the house and reached the back door just as his mother was putting the food on the table.

"Good thing I was expecting you," she laughed as she kissed him. "There's some extra bacon an' coffee, an' it won't take me but a minute to whip up more flapjacks. Here's one o' my fresh-made doughnuts while you're waiting. Pa'll be right down."

The food aboard the *Javelin* had been prepared by amateurs, and Bob hadn't realized how good a home-cooked meal would taste. He thoroughly enjoyed his breakfast, giving the family the news between mouthfuls.

"We'll be towed down to Boston today," he explained. "It shouldn't take too long to fill the hold with cargo an' get a crew shaped up. Then we're off for Californy, an' maybe even China. I doubt if I'll get home again for quite a few months—perhaps a year. By that time I reckon I'll rate as an able seaman."

His father grunted. "From what I hear, Californy's a mighty wicked place," he said. "See you don't get into trouble. Steer clear o' liquor an' women an' gamblers."

"Yes, sir," said Bob, trying not to smile. "I'll be good an' careful. But I doubt if I get ashore in San Francisco more'n once or twice, so you an' Mother don't have to worry too much. You sure you wouldn't like me to bring you a nice big nugget from the gold fields?"

Tobias Wingate snorted. "I've seen some young fools that went out there after gold," he replied. "Generally they come home broke an' whining to their fathers to pay off their debts. I haven't set eyes on a nugget yet."

They sat awhile around the table. Then Bob's father had to go, for he was already late at the ropeworks. Mrs. Wingate promised she would come down to the ferry slip to see the *Javelin* towed down the river.

"I know you'll be a good boy," she told her son. "You always have been. This is a big change in all our lives, but I pray and believe it's for the best."

She hugged him, gave him a paper sack full of doughnuts, and waved good-by as he trudged off to board the ferry.

*　　　*　　　*

The *R. B. Forbes* had brought Mr. Chase and several of his merchant friends from Boston. In addition, there was a band aboard that played almost constantly from the time the steamboat entered the harbor. The music and the general air of excitement had brought hundreds of spectators to the docks and streets overlooking the river.

Bob pushed his way through the crowd by the ferry slip, spotted the *Javelin*'s boat tied to a pier, and made it back to the ship well before the ten o'clock deadline.

The captain was on the quarterdeck now, talking to his

distinguished guests from Boston. The clipper was gay with flags. Her new cordage was taut and her brass and brightwork shone. In spite of the fact that her spars were bare of canvas, she bore herself proudly.

At eleven o'clock the *R. B. Forbes* cast off from the wharf and chugged alongside. The towing cable was passed to the ship and made fast to a bollard at the forepeak. Then the band burst into a fanfare and the captain ordered the clipper's anchor hoisted.

Bob was one of the four seamen who sweated the big hook up, heaving around on the capstan while the bosun bellowed a chantey. The cable came in through an iron-shod hawsehole in the bow, the anchor was catted, and the steam tug picked up the slack in the towline. There was a loud cheer from shore as the *Javelin* started down the Narrows with the ebbing tide.

It was a fine, bright morning. When they cleared New Castle Point, the Isles of Shoals stood out clearly off the port bow, with Boon Island farther away to the northeast. The gentlemen from the city lolled in chairs on the quarter-deck and enjoyed the view, while the course was laid for Cape Ann at a steady six knots.

It was late afternoon when they passed Marblehead Neck, and shore lights were twinkling through the dusk as they threaded between the islands into Boston Bay. By ten o'clock the clipper was tied up at a long wharf on the waterfront.

"If all voyages were that easy," growled Red Gilman, as he changed the watch, "there'd be mighty little use for topmen. Wish we'd had canvas on her today. We'd ha' left that smoke pot of a tugboat a long way astern."

Next morning the sails began to arrive from Colt, the famous sailmaker. They were hauled to the wharf on huge drays, pulled by four horses, for there were literally tons of canvas. Bob felt of the tough, heavy stuff and wondered

how sailormen along the yards could ever handle it in a squall. That was one of the things he would learn before he was much older. Later in the day some of the crew came aboard and the rest of the afterguard reported for duty. Evan Langdon was the first officer. He was a big, quiet man with hair beginning to turn gray. Somewhere along the line he must have missed the promotion that would have made him master of his own ship. But there was no question of his ability.

The second mate was only twenty-one, a young Salem mariner in his fourth year at sea, and headed for the top. He was quick in his judgments, loud-spoken, completely sure of himself. His name was Bill Wyatt. The third mate,

Rodney Snow, was already familiar to Bob. The fourth, George Preble, was even younger than Wyatt. Bob liked his looks at once. He was tall and lanky and talked with a down-East farmer's drawl, but he could move fast when he wanted. Bob learned afterward that Preble came from Kennebunk, in York County, Maine—his own home county.

The men before the mast were a mixed lot. Perhaps twenty of them were real seamen—Norwegians, Swedes, and Danes, with a scattering of hot-headed, foul-mouthed Liverpool Irish who had learned their trade on the packet ships. Others were young landlubbers whose one idea was to get to California and who were willing to sign on early for the chance. The balance of the crew would be recruited later, when the clipper was ready for sea.

One individual Bob was glad to see aboard was the cook. He was a two-hundred-pound Negro named Absalom, a grave-faced, self-respecting man, reputed to be the best ship's cook in any galley. They had a taste of what he could do at suppertime, and it was almost as good a meal as the Kittery lad would have had at home.

While he was standing harbor watch that evening, a carriage and pair came rolling down the wharf. There were three people in the vehicle—a well-dressed man and woman and a young fellow about his own age. After a few fond exchanges of farewells, the boy slung a chest on his shoulder and came aboard. He was sturdy and curly-haired, a little shorter than Bob but strong looking.

"Hi," he greeted Bob cheerfully. "I guess you're the other ship's boy. I heard there'd be two of us. Where do I stow my chest? Name's Matt Ryder, by the way."

"Good to have you aboard," Bob returned with a grin. "I'm Bob Wingate, and I've been expecting you. The bosun says two boys always get in more trouble than one, but at least we'll be company for each other. Let me give you a hand with that box. Have you already signed on?"

Matt said he had, but refused any help in carrying the sea chest. He followed his guide to the forecastle and took the bunk next to Bob's. Then he reported to First Officer Langdon, who had the watch.

"I suppose," said the older man, "I ought to put you in different watches, but I was a ship's boy once myself. Maybe you'll both learn faster if you're together. We'll try it, anyhow."

The two youngsters had a chance to get acquainted that night. Matt's father, Bob gathered, was in the importing business in Boston, a man of some wealth and a friend of Eli Chase. He had expected his son to go to Harvard and then study law. When Matt finally convinced him that he wanted to be a clipper captain instead of a lawyer, Mr. Ryder had persuaded his shipowner friend to give him a taste of sailoring.

"I guess," Matt laughed, "he thinks I'll get all I want of it in one voyage and come back to college. That's where I aim to fool him."

*   *   *

For the better part of two weeks all hands were kept busy bending the new sails to the yards. The *Javelin*, under full canvas, would carry more than thirty sails. There were five square sails on each mast—courses, topsails, topgallant sails, royals, and skysails. Forward there were the three jibs, and aft, the gaff-rigged spanker on the mizzenmast. In addition, she carried studding sails, pronounced "stuns'ls," on the outer ends of the fore and main yards, and big, triangular staysails set on the stays between the masts. Her whole sail area, Bob estimated, would come close to three thousand square yards of canvas.

Working aloft on the yardarms was comparatively easy as long as they lay at the dock, sheltered from the wind. Neither of the ship's boys had any fear of height or were subject to dizziness. Even on the main royal yard, one hundred and forty feet above the deck, Bob soon learned to brace his feet in the footropes, lean well over the top of the spar, and work with both hands, whistling and unconcerned.

Once the sails were made fast to the yards, each was stretched taut to make sure it fitted. Clew lines, buntlines, leech lines, and reef tackles were attached, and the canvas was furled in gaskets.

The work was actually ahead of schedule by the first of August. If her cargo had been ready, the *Javelin* might have sailed only a week or two later. However, most clippers avoided the winter storms off Cape Horn when they could. Spring would be coming in the Southern Hemisphere in October, and a delay at the start might mean a faster voyage. There was another reason why the clipper didn't sail early, but Bob didn't hear about it until the day she put to sea. Meanwhile, he was given shore leave and went to Matt's home for a day and a night.

The Ryder home on Beacon Street was an impressive place. On the outside it was big but plain enough—one of a row of four-story brick dwellings with marble steps. But the interior was an eye opener. It was furnished in the lavish style of mid-century Boston. Rich hangings and carved Chinese chests gave it a look of oriental luxury. Bob had a huge bedroom all to himself and slept in a great four-poster that would have accommodated a whole family.

Matt loaned him a suit of good clothes so that he need not appear at dinner in the dungarees that were all he had in his seabag. The meal was served by two uniformed maids, and as soon as Bob got over his first shyness, he enjoyed it. The Ryders were pleasant, well-bred people who tried to put him at his ease. They asked him about his family, about Portsmouth and Kittery, and led him on to talk of his own ambitions.

When he got on the subject of clipper ships, Bob could talk well. He knew the record voyages of all the fastest ships for the last five years—*Sea Witch, Surprise, Sword-Fish, Flying Fish, Contest, John Gilpin, Oriental.* Every one of them had sailed from New York or Boston to San Francisco in a hundred days or less. And of course there was the matchless record of the great *Flying Cloud*—eighty-nine days around the Horn to the Golden Gate!

Matt's knowledge of the subject was at least equal to Bob's, for he had personally met some of the famous clipper captains. The boys spoke in awed voices of such masters as Philip Dumaresq, Josiah Creesy, Nat Palmer, Edward Nickels, and Robert Waterman.

"I believe," said Bob, "that our own Cap'n Sprague is as good as any of 'em—give him the right ship. He sailed the *Tornado* for two years an' did well with her. But she isn't as big as our *Javelin*—nor as fast."

Mr. Ryder smiled at the last statement. "You boys say 'our' when you talk about the *Javelin* as if you owned her," he said. "That's fine—glad you take pride in your ship. But don't either of you ever worry about what may happen to your beautiful clippers in a few years? The steamboat men are saying the age of sail is about over. If they start putting engines in all the ships, what becomes of your plans to be clipper captains?"

The boys laughed heartily at the idea of sail being replaced.

"It'll be a long time," Matt replied, "before any teakettle of a steamboat can stay within hailing distance of a big square-rigger like the *Javelin*. Sure, I know they've put steam in some o' the Atlantic packets now. But not one of 'em has come close to the fourteen days the *Independence* made from New York to Liverpool, or the sixteen days, westbound against winter gales, that Cap'n Bailey did in the *Yorkshire*. No, Dad, sailing ships are here to stay. Bob and I'll command our own skysail-yarders, never you fear!"

Back aboard, next day, they found the hatches open and cargo going into the hold. Like most of the California clippers of the time, the *Javelin* would be able to clear almost half her original cost in a single voyage to San Francisco. The booming Pacific Coast port was the gateway for all supplies going into the gold fields. Nothing was being manufactured in California and very little food was being raised. The whole population—mostly fortune hunters from all over the world—was engaged in a frenzied search for sudden wealth. As a consequence, the barest necessities of life brought enormous prices.

There were stories of flour selling for $500 a barrel in Sacramento; a keg of nails for $100; shovels and axes, shirts and trousers, for as much as $50 apiece. It was no wonder that New York and Boston merchants were reaping fabulous profits from every clipper voyage.

In the cargo that came aboard the *Javelin* there was a strange assortment of goods, ranging all the way from staples like beans and flour and salt pork to silks and laces for the gay ladies of San Francisco, fine broadcloth and polished boots for the gambling men, sturdy cowhide brogans, denims, and corduroys for the miners. Finally, among the things Bob saw lowered through the hatches, there was a heavy case that held, he was told, a shipment of the new Colt's revolving pistols.

IV

During the last week of August the ship was taken on a three-day shakedown cruise that gave the boys a preliminary taste of real sailoring. Captain Sprague took her out on a day of light westerly breezes, and once outside Boston Light she carried nearly all her canvas. It gleamed bright and new in the sunlight. Off Cape Cod the wind increased, and seamen were sent aloft to take in skysails and royals. It was Bob's first taste of the upper yards at sea, and it gave him a glorious sense of speed and danger. He was on the lee side, helping to furl the foreroyal. From that dizzy height he could look straight down into the frothing waves that swept aft from under the clipper's forefoot.

They ran on southward under shortened sail and by nightfall were a hundred miles or more off the port of New York. Bob and Matt were on watch from eight to midnight. The job assigned them by the first officer was to tend the running lights and keep them filled and trimmed. They were big whale oil lamps with heavy glass shields, mounted well forward on either side.

Bob had the red port light in his charge, and Matt took care of the green one to starboard. They burned steadily, needing little attention. Bob stood by the rail, out of the glare of the light, looking out over the empty darkness of the Atlantic. Under him the ship moved constantly, rising and falling to the rhythm of the swells, her cordage creaking with a contented sound. She was like a live thing that had found her true element at last.

Once, in the final hour of the watch, he saw a tiny red spark far away to leeward. It was the port light of another vessel coming up the coast—perhaps a clipper making for New York after a long voyage. It came no nearer but passed silently astern.

In the morning, somewhere off the Delaware Capes, they brought the ship about. With twenty men at the braces, she was steered up into the wind, and the yards came around smartly. Within two or three minutes the *Javelin* was on a northward reach. The wind shifted more to the north at noon, and once more the yards had to be trimmed. It was all good experience for the greener members of the crew.

They made a sweep to the east to clear Nantucket and Cape Cod, then ran on northeastward through the night. Bob figured they must be nearly to Portland by morning. Once more the ship was brought about, and they made for Boston Harbor. The Kittery boy climbed the rigging, hoping to catch a glimpse of his home shore, but all he could see was a low smudge on the horizon that must have been the Isles of Shoals.

They took a pilot aboard and footed handsomely into port under topsails, with all flags flying. On the quarterdeck Captain Sprague's weatherbeaten face wore a look of satisfaction. Though he said nothing to the crew, they knew he was well pleased with his new ship.

Still more crates and bales were waiting on the wharf. They were stowed in the hold that afternoon, and the next day the steward, who was named Daggett, and Absalom, the cook, went ashore to purchase food for the voyage.

"If they bring any perishable stuff aboard," said Matt, "you can lay to it we're about ready to sail."

It was the next morning when wagonloads of stores began to arrive. First a supply of fresh water was taken aboard, followed by casks of pork and beef and ship biscuit. Then the boys saw apples and potatoes, carrots and other fresh vegetables. Finally some cases of eggs and tinned delicacies were carried aft to the officers' quarters.

"This is it!" cried Matt triumphantly. "Wish I could get a last shore leave tonight, so I could let the folks know we're pulling out."

Bob laughed at him. "I guess your dad knows as well as we do," he said. "Isn't he a shareholder in the *Javelin*? You wait—he'll be here to see us off."

By the time they turned in, everybody aboard knew that tomorrow was sailing day. The mates told off small harbor watches and ordered the rest of the crew to get to sleep.

"It's the last full night's rest ye'll have for better'n three months," the bosun warned them, "an' I want all hands ready to roll out sharp at daybreak."

Falling asleep wasn't as easy as Bob had thought. The excitement of starting his first real voyage made his pulse beat faster, and he tossed restlessly in his bunk for an hour or two. Then, before he knew it, it was morning. The shrilling of the bosun's pipe had him out in jig time, and he lined up beside Matt amidships, where the crew was being mustered. The roll was called. Then the captain addressed them from the quarterdeck.

"Men," he said, "I heard last night that a clipper sailed from New York yesterday. She's the *Goldfinder*—a new ship and a good one. Built by Donald McKay, right here in East Boston. There are some bets being laid that she'll beat us to San Francisco. What's your answer to that?"

"No!" they all roared heartily.

"Good!" said Captain Sprague. "We'll be casting off in two hours' time. Get your breakfasts eaten and look alive. It won't be the captains or the ships—it'll be the smartest crew that wins this race."

An hour later a crowd had begun to assemble on the wharf. Matt pointed to a carriage rolling nearer over the cobbles.

"You were right," he told Bob. "That's my father, sure enough."

Mr. Ryder came aboard, spoke to the first mate, and walked forward to the place where the two boys were stationed.

"A big day!" he said with a smile. "But it'll be an even bigger one when you come safe home. I wanted to wish you both a fine voyage. They tell me there's a race involved."

"There sure is," Matt replied. "If you want to win some money, Dad, put it on the *Javelin*!"

His father laughed. "I'll leave the betting to the young hotheads," he said. "But I've got quite a financial stake in the cargo you're carrying, so take it to California as fast as you can."

He gave Matt a hug, shook Bob's hand, and went back to the pier. Not long after, orders were shouted, the dock lines were cast off, and all hands started making sail. A cheer went up from the crowd on shore as the clipper eased gracefully out into open water. Bob, pulling on the topsail halyards, raised one hand long enough to wave briefly. Then, with the wind bellying her lofty canvas, the clipper began to pick up speed.

*   *   *

The *Javelin* had sailed at ten in the morning. With a fair wind abeam she logged one hundred and sixty miles by midnight and was well out into the Atlantic. Actually, as Bob knew from the charts, Boston was very little farther than New York on the voyage to Cape Horn. If the *Gold-finder* had started at the same hour a day earlier, she would have more easting to make, and was probably still only twenty-four hours ahead. He wondered if they would have a look at their rival soon. It wasn't until weeks later, when they had sailed five thousand miles without sighting a single ship, that he realized how unlikely such a meeting would be.

After the first day, life and work aboard the clipper settled into a regular routine. Fortunately, the weather held fair and the wind steady. That gave the mates time to hammer most of the less experienced crew members into shape. Some were lazy, some were stupid, but they learned in spite of themselves. Discipline was firm to the point of harshness. Red Gilman let them know that orders were to be obeyed and was quite ready to back up his words with a rope's end, a heavy fist, or a belaying pin. And solidly behind his authority stood the mates.

Neither Bob nor Matt had much trouble with the bosun. They were willing and intelligent, and they snapped to it promptly when a command was given. But some of the poor lubbers who had signed on for the ride fared badly. One pasty-faced young Boston clerk named Fansler was miserably seasick for four whole days. When at last Gilman drove him out on deck, he was so weak he could barely stand, let alone bear a hand at the braces. Bob felt sorry for him, but he knew that action and fresh air would cure the fellow faster than sprawling in his bunk.

Others were more actively troublesome. A hulking, black-bearded man known as Grogan was the ringleader of a group that shirked and grumbled most of the time. There were only half a dozen of them, but they did all they could to spread discontent among the rest of the crew.

Grogan was assigned to the same watch as the boys, so they saw a good deal of him, both on deck and in the forecastle. There was no grog served aboard American ships. That was one of the things Grogan griped about, but the ugly-looking Irishman always smelled of liquor. Once Bob saw him sneaking a nip from a squat bottle he had hidden in his sea chest. Bob said nothing about it and hoped the man didn't know he had been observed. Life before the mast was hard enough without having trouble with a fellow like Grogan.

The two ship's boys did the same work as the other sailors on deck and aloft. But, in addition, they were given special tasks that would help in their officers' training. Four days after leaving port they were in the Gulf Stream, not far from Bermuda. The wind was southwesterly, and the ship ran close-hauled under full canvas.

George Preble, the fourth mate, came forward and found the two youngsters sitting on a coil of rope in the shade of the foresail. They were off watch at the time.

"Come along aft," he said. "The skipper says it's time you learned to take the log."

He led the way to the taffrail and showed them a good-sized reel attached there. From it a long line ran out astern, and on the end of the line they could see a quadrant of wood bobbing in the ship's wake.

Preble took a large watch out of his pocket, waited till the second hand marked the beginning of a minute, and released a catch on the side of the reel. At once the line spun out.

"Count the knots," said the young officer.

Every fifty feet there was a bit of white tape tied into a knot in the line. Bob counted aloud as they ran past. At half a minute Preble shut off the reel. "How many?" he asked.

"I made it ten," Bob replied, and Matt nodded agreement.

The fourth mate grinned. "That's all there is to it," he said, reeling in the line once more. "Ten knots it was. That's ten nautical miles an hour. We have to read it every hour an' write it down on the day's log sheet. Old time sailors didn't have any watches, so they used a little sandglass. The sand was supposed to run through in half a minute, but it got slowed up in sticky weather, so they had to make allowances. Any good seaman can come within a knot or so, just by watching the way a ship foots along."

He showed them how he entered the speed on the log sheet in the cabin, then hung the watch on a hook beside it.

"Next time you'll do it while I stand by," he told them. "That'll be at four bells, so look alive."

When four bells struck, they hurried aft and found the young officer waiting for them.

"Here," he said to Matt, "you hold the watch. Put that thong around your neck so you don't drop it overboard. I lost a watch that way when I was a ship's boy an' it cost me most o' my pay for the voyage. You run the reel, Bob, an' do the counting."

They performed the duty to his satisfaction and came up with a speed of nine and a half knots.

"That's good enough going in a medium light wind," Preble commented. "It's an exceptional voyage when you make many days of better'n two hundred sea miles. An' three hundred is somethin' to brag about. I guess the *Flying Cloud* holds the record for a single day's log."

"Right, sir," Bob put in. "She sailed 374 miles in one day."

"In 1851," Matt added, not to be left out. "She had the southeast trades on her tail, an' she was headed north after rounding the Horn."

Preble chuckled. "You lads must ha' been studying up," he said. "Be back in an hour for another go at it."

Several days later they had their first turn at the wheel. They were through the "horse latitudes" now and beginning to pick up the northeast trade winds, so that steering wasn't too difficult. Even so, it was a couple of hours before Bob, under the bosun's schooling, was able to hold the great, plunging vessel on her course. The secret, he was told, was to keep one eye on the set of the sails and one on the compass heading.

"The rest," said Gilman, "ye do by feel. After a bit yer hands can tell in a second if ye're givin' her too much rudder. A ship's as touchy as a young girl. Have to be gentle with her, but plenty firm, too."

When both Bob and Matt were able to take their regular trick at the wheel, Evan Langdon, the first mate, began giving them easy lessons in navigation. They were introduced to the ship's charts—not only the regular ones but the new wind and current charts designed by Lieutenant Matthew Maury of the U. S. Navy and now coming into general use.

"Only a handful o' clippers had Maury's charts a year 'ago," said Langdon. "Now a lot o' the best masters use 'em. I reckon the *Goldfinder* has 'em, too. If not, we're lucky. They're pretty sure to give an advantage of four or five days on a long voyage."

Each day at noon, by the big chronometer in the cabin, the first mate shot the sun. The sextant gave him its exact altitude, and by means of a few calculations he could establish the ship's latitude and longitude. On days of rain or heavy clouds their position had to be figured by dead reckoning—taking the number of miles covered since the last sight and allowing for probable drift.

All this was hard for the boys to grasp at first, but they were eager to learn. Matt, who was quicker than Bob at figures, mastered the calculating part a day before his friend. After that their progress was about equal. Celestial navigation—determining position by the stars—would come later, when they had spent perhaps a year at sea.

For the most part the wind and weather had been fine so far. But on the twentieth day out of Boston the breeze dropped and the sea, clear to the horizon, lay flat and glassy under the broiling sun. They had entered the doldrums. When Langdon took his sight at noon, the sweat ran down into his eyes. He worked out the position and announced it to Bob, who stood by.

"Two degrees, thirty minutes, north," he said. "And an even thirty west. Not far from St. Paul's Rocks. Maybe we'll sight 'em tomorrow, but I hope the drift sets the other way."

The air in the forecastle was stifling that night, and most of the watch stretched out on deck to sleep. After an hour Bob decided he would be more comfortable if he had a blanket under him. He groped his way inside, where the only light came from a smoky oil lamp hanging above the table. A movement in the shadows made him pause. Then he went to his berth, got the blanket, and went out again.

"Matt," he whispered, as he lay down beside his chum, "do you keep anything valuable in your sea chest?"

The other boy sat up quickly. "Why?" he asked.

"I thought," said Bob, "I saw somebody sneaking away from your bunk when I went in. I wasn't sure, but it could have been Grogan."

V

Matt jumped to his feet. "I guess the only thing worth stealing would be my wallet," he said with a frown. "I had a few dollars of my own, and Mother gave me twenty-five in bills when I left. I don't carry it around on me—it's in the bottom of the chest, under my sea boots. Come on—let's look!"

Together they tiptoed into the dimly lit crew's quarters. It smelled, as usual, of dirty clothes, unwashed bodies, and stale pipe smoke. Bob went on past the table, peering into bunks. If there had been anyone there earlier, there was certainly no sign of him now. He came back to join Matt, where he knelt beside the open sea chest.

"Empty!" the Boston boy exclaimed under his breath. "Here's the wallet, all right, but the money's gone!"

"Then I really did see somebody move," said Bob. "He's gone now—must have ducked out right after I left. Gee, Matt, I'm sorry! If I'd had any sense, I'd have stayed here till he showed himself."

"Well," his friend told him, "don't let it bother you. Money's no good to me aboard ship anyhow. I just don't like the idea of having a thief around."

"Think we ought to tell one o' the mates?" Bob asked.

Matt shook his head. "I'd rather not," he said. "Maybe we can catch him ourselves. From now on we'll keep an eye on Grogan—the dirty scum!"

They went out into the heavy night air again. In the tangle of bodies that lay snoring on the deck, it was impossible to tell one man from another, so they returned to their places and soon went to sleep themselves. It wasn't until later, when the watch was changed, that Bob caught the reek of whisky and saw Grogan slouching past.

Dawn came at last, but it brought no wind with it. The sun popped out of the eastern sea like a great ball of molten metal, and before it was an hour high, the heat was stifling. On both sides of the ship lay streaks and patches of brownish yellow weed that moved listlessly on the slow, oily swells. There were tiny marine things crawling or swimming in the weed, and occasionally a little flying fish broke the surface to whir along for a few yards and re-enter the water with a splash.

The sailors were grumpy and morose. Tempers flared in the heat and several fights broke out, stopped only by the quick action of the mates.

Twice that morning they felt a brief puff of air, and all hands were rushed to the braces to square the drooping sails around. Then the wind died again. At noon the first mate took his bearings and reported a drift to the south and west. They had moved twenty or thirty miles in a day.

"Gosh," said Matt fervently, "I sure hope the *Goldfinder* got becalmed, too!"

Late in the afternoon clouds formed overhead and a sudden shower poured straight down on the ship, sluicing the sails and decks with tepid water. They stood there dripping, catching drinks in their open mouths. It was too warm to be refreshing, but it tasted better than the stuff pumped from the iron tank into the scuttle butt each morning.

The rain lasted only a few minutes. When it had passed, some of the sailors baited hooks and fished over the rail. For a while the only thing they caught was one little dog-shark. Then suddenly a school of small, fat fish began to strike the bait. Nobody knew what they were called, but within ten minutes half a hundred of them had been hauled aboard. They were striped black and white and averaged a pound or two apiece.

"You wan' 'em cooked fo' supper," Absalom announced, "you gotta clean 'em fust."

The fish chowder he prepared that night was a welcome change from the "salt horse," beans and hardtack that formed the bulk of their diet. Once again it was too hot to sleep inside. Bob lay forward, propped against the capstan, and watched the stars sweep overhead—no longer the familiar constellations of home, but strange new galaxies for which he had no names.

Sometime in the first watch after midnight there was a stirring of canvas and a creak of cordage.

"All hands to man the braces!" Gilman bellowed. "Heave, boys, an' haul 'em 'round. It's the southeast trades!"

The breeze freshened and the tall ship heeled to starboard. All that day she beat to the southward, logging eight to ten knots, and in the night she crossed the line. There was no ceremony to mark the occasion—no horseplay with King Neptune and Davy Jones giving an initiation to greenhorns. But Bob looked off to the south and nudged his companion.

"Matt," he said, "see those bright stars down close to the horizon? Make a sort of a cross, don't they? I bet that's it— the Southern Cross!"

Matt stared and agreed. "That means we're shellbacks for sure!" he chuckled. "Nobody can ever call us lubbers again!"

*　　*　　*

The *Javelin* had crossed the equator when she was twenty-two days out—by no means a record, but fair enough considering the fact she had lain becalmed. There was no way to tell where the *Goldfinder* might be, but Captain

Sprague sailed his ship as if he believed his rival was far ahead. Even when the southeast trades blew their strongest, he kept her under topgallants, and at any sign of lighter winds he ordered royals set.

They went roaring down the coast of Brazil, logging close to three hundred miles a day, and were off the River Plate on the tenth of October. Only once in all that time did they sight another sail. It was ahead, five or six miles away on the starboard bow, and they were overhauling it. For a few minutes there was excitement aboard the *Javelin,* for many thought they had overtaken the New York clipper. But when they brought her abeam, she turned out to be a bluff-bowed, stumpy-masted New Bedford whaler, wallowing along under topsails.

"Maybe we'll hail her," Bob suggested. "Find out if she's sighted the *Goldfinder.*"

But the skipper had no such idea. He drove the *Javelin* swiftly past the other ship, leaving her far to leeward. Within half an hour they were alone again in the vast emptiness of the South Atlantic.

Keeping an eye on Grogan wasn't as easy as it had sounded. The Liverpool Irishman was an expert at dropping out of sight, especially if there was work to be done. Not that he was afraid of dangerous jobs. Bob had seen him reefing aloft on the footropes of the skysail yard with the wind howling past at forty miles an hour. What Grogan avoided was the everyday drudgery of hauling braces and scrubbing decks.

"You know," Matt told his friend one night when they were far up in the bows, away from the rest of the crew, "I believe he's got a secret hiding place. We're six weeks out o' port an' he still seems to get plenty o' liquor. He could never have smuggled that much aboard in his sea chest."

"Yes, but where?" Bob replied. "It couldn't be in the fo'c's'le."

"How about the boats?" asked Matt. "Are you game to take a look?"

The clipper carried four boats. Aft were the captain's launch and the jollyboat, and they could be written off. That was officers' country. The longboat and a big whaleboat were lashed in chocks just abaft the mainmast and covered with tarpaulins to keep out rain and spray.

"All right," Bob whispered, after a moment's hesitation. "I'll try the whaleboat. Keep watch an' whistle 'Yankee Doodle' if anybody comes by."

He worked around to the outer side of the boat, squeezed himself up between the strakes and the rail, and unfastened two of the grommets that held the tarpaulin in place. In a minute or two he had wriggled under the flap. It was pitch dark. He lighted a lucifer match and crawled aft over the thwarts. The boat was provisioned, of course, for use in case of shipwreck, but the water casks and food canisters were all tight and in order. Within five minutes he had explored the craft thoroughly. Then, as there was no warning whistle from Matt, he got out the same way he had entered, fastening the tarp once more.

When he had rejoined the other boy, Bob shook his head. "If he's got a hide-out, it isn't in there," he whispered. "You want to try the longboat now?"

Before Matt could answer, the bosun called the watch to man the braces, and the search had to be postponed. For the next few days the crew seemed to be kept busy night and day. They were in the southern horse latitudes, and the weather had grown freaky. Sometimes the yards had to be shifted three or four times in an hour, and they were constantly setting or taking in sail.

In spite of variable winds, the clipper continued to make good days' runs. On October 22 she reached latitude 50° South, and the next morning they sighted the Falklands right abeam. The air had grown colder in the last week, and the boys were glad to wrap up in reef coats when they stood watch.

"This isn't bad," Fourth Mate Preble commented when he saw Bob shivering. "Last time I rounded the Horn, it was in July—middle o' winter. We had icicles hangin' from our noses, an' all the riggin' was inches thick with ice. This is spring, down here. Not much colder'n Maine or Nova Scotia."

With every hour that brought them nearer to Cape Horn, the temperature dropped and the wind increased. They needed no fix of the sun to tell them they had reached the "howling fifties."

Now, still in the lee of a bleak land shown on the charts as Tierra del Fuego, they found the gales from the west blowing so strongly that Captain Sprague had the topgallant sails reefed. Working up there on the fore-topgallant yard, Bob was hampered by numb, half-frozen hands and buffeted by winds that almost tore him from the footrope. Yet a strange, wild exuberance filled him. He had heard it said that a Cape Horn voyage separated the men from the boys. He was a man now, and his bleeding hands proved it.

Bob realized, as he came down the ratlines, that Grogan had not been with the rest of the watch aloft on the yards. It seemed unusual, for the Irishman rarely shirked duty of that kind. As he staggered aft, Bob's mind was on other things, but he noticed suddenly that Grogan was there in front of him, moving toward the lee rail. The man seemed to have materialized out of nowhere.

For a moment Bob thought he must have been mistaken —that the fellow must have been aloft after all, possibly in the main top. Then his eye fell on the carpenter's cuddy. It was a little structure just aft of the scuttle butt. The door wasn't closed tightly but swung in the wind, as if someone had forgotten to shut it. With one eye on Grogan, whose back was turned, the boy reached the cuddy quickly and

peered inside. He saw the usual array of tools in racks on the bulkheads. But for the first time he noticed something else. There was a small hatchway inside, in the deck. Not over three feet square, it had a ring in the hatch cover that looked as if it had been frequently used.

After that one glance Bob pulled the door tight, latching it, then went on about his business. He didn't believe Grogan had seen him.

The seas were running higher now, and the ship took a lot of white water aboard as she smashed through them. With all hands constantly working at the braces, it was impossible to keep dry. Bob was drenched and shivering, and the hard physical effort was all that kept him warm. Between times, when a wave came aboard, he hung on as best he could to the rigging or a hand rope. Often Matt was beside him, but they had no breath to talk.

At last the end of the watch came, and they were allowed to go inside. Hot soup and coffee were going around.

"Git yo'selfs warmed up," said the grinning Absalom as he filled their tin cups. "Nex' watch yo'll need it. Goin' to git wuss befo' it gits better."

"I reckon he's right," Bob told Matt between chattering teeth. "The way the skipper's driving her, we'll be heading 'round the Horn itself before morning."

He pulled his chum off into a corner while they sipped the steaming soup. "Maybe I've found out where Grogan hides," he whispered. "There's a little hatch inside the carpenter's cuddy. Chips may be in on it with him. Or else he sneaks down there when Chips is busy."

"Old Johnson wouldn't have anything to do with a rat like him," Matt replied. "If Grogan's using that hatch, he must be doing it without Chips's knowing. You'd think the mates would be wise to him."

Bob had warmed up enough to grin. "I guess he turns his head the other way or holds his breath when they're around," he said. "O' course he never acts drunk, but the bosun must suspect, if he ever gets within wind of him."

They started for their bunks, but before they could lie down, the whole crew was ordered on deck.

"All hands aloft!" shouted Red Gilman. "Haul on the buntlines and clew lines and furl the courses and to'gallants."

The ship was making heavy weather of it now. As Bob climbed the fore shrouds, he was pitched violently from side to side with the swaying of the mast. Below him the deck was awash in crashing seas that came over the starboard bow. They must be out of the lee of the land now, for the wind hit them with full gale force. No sooner had the boy reached the topgallant yard than driving particles of sleet filled the air. They stung his face like bullets, but he bent his head and strained doggedly to knot the gaskets.

Behind him he heard a ripping sound above the uproar of the wind. Glancing aft, he saw the main topgallant sail torn clear of the yard and whipping crazily. Then there came a long, piercing scream and something limp and dark went pinwheeling toward the deck, far below. He had seen his first man die at sea.

VI

Bob felt his stomach turn over, but he gritted his teeth and worked with his mates on the yard till they finished their job. Then, weak with terror, he made his way slowly down the ratlines.

The man who had fallen from the main top was no longer on the deck. He had been carried aft to the cabin. Bob heard that it was Fansler, the young greenhorn who had shipped in order to reach California. Losing his hold when the sail went out, he had landed head first, breaking his neck.

With two men straining to hold the wheel, the *Javelin* plunged on southward under topsails. Inside the forecastle Bob flung himself into his bunk, wet clothes and all, and slept, exhausted, for two hours. Then the watch was called out once more.

The force of the wind had fallen a little, though the seas still ran mountain high. Twice, clinging to the lifelines with all his strength, Bob had his feet washed right out from under him by the rush of a wave. One of the boats had been battered off its chocks and now blocked the passage on the starboard side of the waist. With every sea that came aboard it crashed to and fro, threatening to break such lashings as still held it.

"Ryder—Wingate! Here and lend a hand!" the second mate yelled. As the boys scrambled aft, they saw him throw the bight of a heavy rope over the thrashing longboat's bow. Between two waves he bent a quick reef knot and flung the free end of the rope to Bob.

The boy needed no order. There was a big iron cleat by the rail, and he jumped forward, passing the rope around it. With Matt's help he began to haul, snubbing the boat little by little to starboard. Several times the wash of the seas wrenched the unwieldy craft almost out of their grip, but they hung on. At last they had the bow wedged close to the cleat and Wyatt made it fast.

By the time daylight came they were able to take stock of the damage done. Some of the longboat's planking had been splintered, but the hull could be patched up. In addition to the main topgallant sail one of the jibs had carried away and some of the running rigging had been torn out of the blocks. Absalom, the cook, was unhappy because he had lost his chicken coop. The little structure, with the dozen fowls it held, was washed overboard in the first onset of the gale.

Bit by bit the violence of the wind and waves abated. At noon the dead seaman was sent over the side, wrapped in a piece of sailcloth, and Captain Sprague read the brief burial service while the silent crew stood by. Then all hands were sent aloft again to shake out the courses and repair damage to the running gear. It was still blowing too hard to carry anything above the topsails, but a new main topgallant was bent on and furled.

Doggedly the clipper bucked ahead all day, making a speed of four or five knots despite headwinds and a strong eastward drift. Bob knew by heart the story of the *Flying Cloud*'s famous voyage in 1851. He remembered she had taken a bad beating off the Horn after losing her main topmast, yet she had made the distance from 50° South in the Atlantic to 50° South in the Pacific in only seven days. He wondered whether the *Javelin* had a chance to do as well.

Matt was evidently thinking along the same lines. "What was today—the twenty-seventh, wasn't it?" he asked his friend that night. "And we're still trying to make our westing. We'll never reach the 50th parallel in two more days —not unless the skipper's willing to crowd on sail."

"I know," Bob agreed. "We only logged about a hundred and ten miles today. But he's on the quarterdeck now, checking the wind. I wouldn't be surprised if we got an order for more canvas pretty quick."

The words were barely out of his mouth when Wyatt hurried forward. "All hands!" he shouted. "Port watch aloft—an' get the sta'board watch on deck!"

The boys scurried up the rigging to their usual station in the foretop. Within a minute they were casting off the gaskets, and the loosened sail flapped and thundered until men below sheeted the sail down. Soon all three topgallant sails were set and drawing.

An hour later the helm was put over as they hauled the yards around. The new course was west by north. A ragged cheer went up from the crew, for they knew "Cape Stiff" was behind them at last.

The twenty-eighth dawned clear, with a fresh westerly wind that sang in the taut stays and shrouds. Royals and skysails were set. Then the watch on deck was put to holystoning and setting the ship to rights. When Bob took the log, he made a count of better than seventeen knots and couldn't believe his eyes. Worried, he checked the watch once more and let the reel run. This time he had asked Matt to join him.

"Seventeen an' a half!" cried the Boston boy. "What did you count?"

"The same," Bob told him. "But, golly! That's sure moving!"

They hurried to Langdon with the report. He looked at

them dubiously and shook his head. "Thought you'd learned to count by now," he said. "Maybe I'd better take it myself."

But when he returned, his face wore a surprised look. "Can't make a liar out o' you," he said. "It's mighty close to eighteen knots! Fastest I ever traveled in any ship. Got to tell Cap'n Sprague, an' I reckon his eyes'll pop!"

It grew squally as the day wore on, and a gust ripped away the fore skysail. At once the other skysails were ordered in, and before nightfall the royals followed. With seas running higher, the decks were awash once more. But still the *Javelin* sped on, logging between twelve and fifteen knots. Trying to figure out the dead reckoning, Bob and Matt decided they must have covered three hundred and sixty sea miles in the last twenty-four hours.

The squalls were gone by morning, and the wind was working around to the southwest, right abeam. Again royals and skysails were spread. The ship rushed forward, heeled so far to starboard that it was hard for the seamen to keep their footing on the canted deck.

After Langdon took his twelve o'clock shot of the sun the word went out officially. The *Javelin* had sailed 366 miles between noon and noon—probably the second fastest day's run ever recorded by a clipper! Only the *Flying Cloud,* in almost the same latitude and longitude, had beaten that mark with 374 miles.

"Where's the *Goldfinder* now?" Matt asked jubilantly. "If she hit the same weather we did coming 'round the Horn, I bet she's a long way astern."

For the past three or four days the boys had been too busy to pay much attention to Grogan. He always appeared when the roll of the watch was called, and Bob had seen him working daringly at the tip of the yardarm during the hazardous job of shifting sails. But when the decks were being scrubbed, he took his bucket and brush and simply slipped out of sight.

Late that afternoon, Bob was reminded of the black-bearded sailor once more. On his hands and knees he was swabbing the deck near the foot of the mainmast when he noticed Grogan standing with bucket in hand, leaning against the carpenter's cuddy. The boy wondered where Chips was. He heard hammering and looked around to find the carpenter mending the broken strakes of the longboat. When he turned his head again, there was no longer any sign of Grogan.

Acting on impulse, Bob made sure nobody else was watching him and darted over to the cuddy. Quietly he opened the door a crack and looked in. He was just in time to see the hatch cover settling into place. In a corner stood the bucket.

The boy went back to his work, but he was certain now that he had been right about Grogan's hide-out. At the change of the watch he hurried to whisper his news to Matt. Together they formed a plan. Later that night, when they were off watch, Bob made certain Grogan was safely in his bunk. Then he stole out and met his chum by the cuddy. There was no lock on the door and the hasp wasn't even in the staple. In a moment they were inside, closing the door after them.

By the light of a match Bob heaved the hatch cover up. They peered down into the dark of the hold and saw the tops of hogsheads four or five feet below.

"Come on," said Matt. "I bet I can find my way around without a light."

But with the match extinguished, they could only grope along the top of the cargo in pitch blackness.

"We've got to have a light," Bob whispered, "or we'll never find anything down here."

"All right," said Matt. "Better be careful, though. I expect there's a lot of stuff down here that would burn like tinder."

They crawled well over to the port side before Bob struck another match. As he did so, there was an exclamation from Matt.

"Look!" he said. "A regular nest!"

Snuggled against the timbers of the ship's side was a rumpled blanket, surrounded by more than a dozen empty bottles. When they pulled back one edge of the blanket, they found where the bottles had come from—a case of whisky. That much they had expected. But a more important discovery awaited them. There was another case there, its lid pried loose. Bob raised it a little, and they stared at the glinting steel of big Colt's revolvers. At least one of them was gone! At that moment the match went out. In the dead air of the hold there had come a sudden draft.

"Quick!" Bob whispered. "He's coming—get away from here!"

Silent as cats they scrambled off in different directions. Bob went forward. When he was twenty feet away from the blanket, he waited, breathless, for a sound. He heard the faint creak of the hatch cover closing, then a stealthy shuffle of feet over the barrel tops. If a light was struck, he was pretty sure he and Matt would be seen, and he wondered how much chance they would have against the brawny Irishman.

Apparently, however, the intruder knew his way well enough in the dark. The shuffling noise went straight to the blanket, and after a moment Bob heard the pop of a cork, followed by a gurgling gulp. The drinker belched contentedly.

Careful not to make a sound, Bob crept across one hogshead, then another. At last his hand touched the clammy iron of the water tank, and he knew where he was. The hatch was less than ten feet to the right. He crouched there, debating whether to wait for Grogan to leave or make a break for it. His decision was to stay. Otherwise, he might put Matt in danger, and he had a feeling Grogan was quite capable of murder.

At that moment his ears caught the sound of breathing, only a yard away. He was sure the bearded sailor was still busy with his bottle and this could only be Matt. Gently he thrust out his arm along the afterside of the tank. His fingers touched flesh, and he heard a half-smothered gasp of surprise.

"It's me—Bob!" he breathed, so softly he wasn't sure the other boy could hear. Then his fingers were gripped by Matt's. He inched along till his lips were right at his friend's ear.

"Come on," he whispered. "We can get out before he knows who we are."

Together they crept aft till they were under the hatch. Bob reached up and felt the lower side of the cover. Then, with a quick movement, he pushed it upward, caught the edge of the coaming, and jerked himself up through the hole. He gave Matt a hand up, and in an instant they dropped the cover in place again, to the accompaniment of muffled curses from below.

The boys shut the cuddy door and raced forward to their bunks. Three minutes later, when Grogan came stumbling into the forecastle, they were wrapped in their blankets, pretending to be as sound asleep as the rest of the watch.

Routed out again before dawn, they came on deck shivering. South of the 40th parallel it was still chilly until the sun came up. Aft by the wheel Bob saw the first mate with his eye on the binnacle, checking the course with the steersman.

"Matt," he said, "I think it's time for us to tell Langdon

what's going on. It's not just a matter of a man's having liquor aboard, or even stealing your money. He's broken into the ship's cargo. And if he's got a gun, he might even be planning a mutiny."

The Boston boy agreed, and they approached the first officer together. "Mr. Langdon," said Bob, "could we have a word with you?"

Langdon eyed him sharply. "Anything wrong?" he asked. "I was just about to take the log. Come on aft with me."

By the taffrail they were well out of earshot of the man at the wheel.

"Maybe you've noticed, sir," said Bob, "that Grogan's about half drunk most o' the time."

"Grogan? You mean that surly fellow with the black whiskers? I knew he was a shirker, but I hadn't realized he was drinking. Where's he keep it?"

"That's just it, sir," Matt put in. "It's part o' the cargo. We think he stole about thirty dollars I had in my sea chest, so we've been watching him. Last night we found he was sneaking down into the hold through the hatch in Chips's cuddy. Bob and I went down there. You ought to take a look yourself, sir. He's all fixed up with a blanket and a big case o' liquor. And he's opened up another case with pistols in it."

Langdon's face had a black look, and he squared his shoulders. "Thanks," he said gruffly. "I'll see to it."

He handed the watch to Bob and motioned to the log reel before he strode off. They saw him go at once to the cabin and reappear with a lantern. Then, while they counted off the knots in the log line, he went forward to the carpenter's cuddy.

"Whew!" breathed Matt. "I hope Grogan's not down there. If he is, there'll be a fight, and I've got a hunch he's handy with a knife."

After five minutes Langdon reappeared. He was alone,

much to the relief of the boys. They met him near the wheel on his return.

"Ten and a half knots, sir," said Bob, putting the watch in the mate's hand.

Langdon beckoned them farther aft. "I found everything just as you reported," he told them. "Two pistols are gone, but I doubt if he's located the ammunition. If I were you, I'd say nothing about this to anyone. Not until we've made sure of the guilty man and put him in irons."

"Ay, ay, sir," they replied in chorus. It was dawn now, and they went forward to put out the running lights. At the change of the watch they got breakfast and returned to their berths for a nap. Bob didn't know how long he had slept, but it could have been only a few minutes when he woke. The forecastle seemed to be empty. He wondered sleepily if all hands had been called on deck and he had somehow missed the order. Hastily he sat up and started pulling on his boots. And at that instant an ugly, bearded face appeared from nowhere.

VII

"Lie still, ye young spalpeen," snarled Grogan. "An' keep yer trap shut or I'll carve the liver out o' yez!"

The man had a knife in his hand—a long seaman's dirk with a glittering blade. His face came closer, and Bob could smell the fumes of whisky on his breath.

"Now," said Grogan, his voice dropping to a menacing whisper, "what were yez doin' in the carpenter's shack? Tell me no lies, or ye'll be dead in the next minute!"

Bob made no answer. He cowered back in his bunk as if he had been frightened speechless. But he was thinking hard. The door of the forecastle stood open. There must be somebody on deck, not too far away.

Suddenly he brought his booted foot up into the Irishman's stomach, and with the other foot he kicked hard at the hand that held the knife. Then, twisting quickly, he leaped out of the bunk and darted for the door, yelling for help.

Behind him he heard the gasping grunt of a man with his wind knocked out. Then George Preble was there in the doorway. The young fourth mate had a belaying pin in his hand. As Bob ducked past him, he saw Preble's arm go up and heard a hollow *thwack* that sounded like a pumpkin being smashed.

The boy scrambled outside and found Wyatt and Gilman waiting there, both armed with clubs. The bosun grinned at him.

"Had to do it this way to catch him," he said. "We wouldn't ha' let him cut ye up."

Beyond them was Matt, pale-faced and gripping a marlinespike.

"A fine friend you are!" Bob laughed shakily. "Wouldn't stay by to help me out!"

Matt shook his head. "It was the mates' idea, not mine," he explained. "I wanted 'em to let me be the bait, but they wouldn't have it. When Gilman roused out the rest o' the watch, I had to come with 'em. You didn't get hurt any, did you?"

"No," said Bob, trying not to let his knees wobble. "It was sort o' close, though. That knife—ugh!"

Preble came out on deck, dragging the unconscious Grogan. Blood was running from a welt on the man's head.

"Reckon he isn't dead," said the Maine man laconically. "Skull's too thick to break."

The others went to Grogan's sea chest and unearthed the two revolvers and thirty-one dollars in bills.

"Look 'em over," Wyatt suggested to Matt. "That's about what was stolen out o' your wallet, isn't it?"

The Boston boy examined the money. "Well," he said, "I can't be sure it's the same money, o' course. But it's about the right amount."

"Keep it," said Wyatt. "He won't be needing it, that's sure."

There was no regular doctor aboard, but Langdon was a fairly competent hand with wounds. He examined Grogan's head, brought him to with a dram of brandy, and bandaged his skull. Then the troublemaker was put in irons and locked securely in the brig.

*　　*　　*

That day they had powerful southerly winds that drove the tall-masted ship forward like a race horse. Sprague kept full canvas on her until sometime in the first dog watch, when a sudden squall came up astern and whipped away the mizzen topgallant mast. Up to that time they had been logging fifteen knots or more, hour after hour.

A score of men hurried aloft to take in the main and fore skysails and royals. Meanwhile, some of the ablest hands were clearing the mizzen wreckage. When Bob came down from the foremast yards and went aft to take the log, he overheard a discussion on the quarterdeck.

"We could make Valparaiso in a day's sail," Langdon was saying. "Likely we'd be able to get a new spar on her in another day an' be on our way."

Sprague rubbed his chin and looked at the weather. "What do you say, Mr. Wyatt?" he asked.

"I'm for going straight on," the second mate replied bluntly. And both Snow and Preble nodded their agreement with him.

"Think you can fish a jury spar that'll hold?" the captain asked them, and again the three junior officers nodded.

"All right," said Langdon with a shrug and a grin. "You've outvoted me—an' I admit it's a shame to lose any o' this breeze."

"It's settled, then," Sprague told them. "Wyatt an' Preble, I'll ask you to find a jury to'gallant mast an' get it up first thing tomorrow. The carpenter'll give you what you need."

Bob was glad. He might have enjoyed a sight of the Chilean seaport—or any land, for that matter. But their race with the *Goldfinder* seemed far more important just now. If the wind held, he thought they might log another big day's run.

By the next noon a tall, slim spar had been selected from the pile lashed on deck. The carpenter squared the heel and cut the fid and sheave holes. It was hoisted up through the topmast trestle trees and cap where the standing rigging was attached, and then it was hauled up to its full height and the running rigging rove off.

When the first mate took his sights, he gave their position as 34° South and 80° West. They had covered 358 nautical miles in the past twenty-four hours and saved at least two days by making their repairs at sea.

That afternoon the wind slacked a little and showers of rain drove down on the ship. Bob and Matt helped rig spare sails to catch the fresh water and sluice it into the tank. Then, stripped to their dungarees, they stood happily and let the cool rain pour into their mouths. It was a grand feeling to be clean again, for many days had passed since they had been able to wash in anything but sea water.

The intermittent showers lasted through that day and part of the next. Then they picked up the steady southeast trades and bowled along northwestward under sunny skies, logging good runs day after day. It was the second week in November when the wind grew fitful again, and the heat of the noon sun beat down on them like a blast from an oven.

On the sixteenth they crossed the equator once more, somewhere to the east of the Galápagos Islands. Matt, who knew every day's entry in the log of the *Flying Cloud,* began calculating their progress with growing excitement. He showed his figures to Bob.

"Captain Creesy was seventy days to the Line," he said, "and we're only seventy-one. The *Cloud* lost a couple of upper masts, too, an' refused to put into Valparaiso, just like we did. I guess there's no chance of our topping her record, but we could be close! How'd you like to be able to brag you'd been on the second fastest voyage ever made in a clipper?"

"Sure I'd like it," said Bob. "But the time to do our bragging is *after* we've made the voyage. Suppose we loaf around in the doldrums like this for a week. We'd be lucky to reach San Francisco in under a hundred days—good enough, I'll grant you—but nothing much to crow about."

Fortunately, his gloomy weather forecast was proved wrong. After a single day of relative calm, the ship picked up a fair breeze from the northeast, right on her starboard beam. Once more she footed fast, under all the canvas she could carry.

For the next two weeks they had ideal sailing weather. Day after day the *Javelin* made good runs, cutting the blue Pacific. First they were off the Gulf of Panama, then the long Central American coastline. After that, Bob could look to windward and tell himself that the mountains of Mexico lay beyond the horizon. And at last they were skirting the great peninsula of Baja California.

Lookouts were posted at the fore and main mastheads now. Some of the crew found it boring duty, but Bob and Matt were eager to go aloft. On the eighty-eighth day out of Boston, it was Bob's turn to scale the ratlines to the fore-topmast crosstrees. He got a leg over the yard and made himself comfortable. Then, with a good view under the straining foot of the topgallant sail, he stared out across a great arc of wind-tossed sea.

To relieve the monotony, he pretended he was in the crow's nest of a whaler and squinted his eyes to pick up the bushy white plume that would mark a spout. Once he really saw one, not half a mile away. The little cloud of steam and spray lasted only a few seconds. Then a long black bulk showed momentarily above the waves and the whale dove again with a splash of its huge tail flukes.

So fascinated had the boy become in watching this performance that he almost missed something far more important. Lifting his eyes to the western horizon, he caught a tiny glint of white. At once he crawled higher to the topgallant yard, trying for a better view. Then he was sure.

"Sail, ho!" he yelled out. "Four points on the port bow. It's the upper sails of a full-rigged ship!"

Matt echoed the hail from the main top. A moment later Wyatt came swarming up to join Bob. He had a telescope on a lanyard around his neck, and now he focused it on the distant speck.

"Clipper-rigged," he murmured excitedly. "And she's on the same course we are. From her new canvas she could be the *Goldfinder*!

He hurried back to the deck, and within five minutes the crew had been rushed aloft to spread studding sails and staysails. Heeled far over to leeward, the *Javelin* ran like a frightened deer, every yard of canvas straining to the utmost.

Somewhat to Bob's disappointment he was relieved from lookout duty, and George Preble went aloft in his place. Every few minutes he reported developments to the deck.

"We've gained on her," he would call. "Now she's breaking out stuns'ls. Must have sighted us."

By the time darkness fell, the two clippers were running almost abreast of each other and only three or four miles apart. Captain Sprague and the mates were now in unanimous agreement that the other vessel was the *Goldfinder*. As Langdon put it, "You can always tell a McKay-built ship. There's something extra sassy about the rake of her masts."

Occasionally, in other latitudes, the *Javelin* had shortened sail at night. Not so that evening. Long after her rival had disappeared in the darkness, she roared on her way with cordage stretched almost to the breaking point.

Bob and Matt had the last watch before dawn. Tending his port running light while the night was still black and the stars bright in the windy sky, Bob looked aft and saw a twinkling spark of green, far off on the horizon. As soon as he was sure it was there, he ran aft and reported to Snow, who had the deck.

Using a night glass, the third mate studied the tiny, flickering dot. "You're dead right, lad," he said happily. "That's her starboard light an' we've laid her well astern!"

At eight bells the boys went off watch but not to bed. They stood at the leeward rail watching the stars fade and the sky grow pale. Gradually, out at the dim, far edge of the sea, they made out topsails beginning to catch the morning light. Already the other clipper was hull down, five or six miles behind and to leeward. They lost her before noon.

That day, their eighty-ninth since clearing from Boston, the bearings showed they were 36°, 10′ North and 123° West. Eagerly Bob read the chart and rushed to tell Matt that the Golden Gate was only a hundred and fifty miles ahead.

"Hey!" cried Matt. "If we could get in tonight, we'd tie the *Flying Cloud*'s record! Come on, wind—blow harder!"

Every hour they took the log, gloating when it was up to fifteen knots, gloomy when it fell below. The officers and many of the foremast hands shared their excitement. Captain Sprague paced back and forth on the quarterdeck, his rough-hewn face unchanged but an impatient quickness in his step.

At six o'clock that evening the wind shifted northerly and grew lighter and more fitful. That was to be expected so close to land, but it slowed the clipper's speed. Before dusk they sighted the South Farallones off the port bow. It was almost time to pick up a pilot, and all hands watched eagerly for the first sign of the cutter's sails.

Then, just as they sighted the peak of Mt. Tamalpais through the gathering dark, a gray bank of fog shut down over the coast. There was nothing to do but heave to until morning. Bitterly disappointed, Bob lay in his bunk and listened to the doleful note of the fog bell and the wet slatting of the sails as the ship rocked to the swell.

The fog blew away before dawn. In the first light the lookout announced two sails, and everybody crowded to the rails. The *Javelin* had steerageway now and was bowling along on an easterly course. Five miles or so astern they could see the other clipper approaching under a press of canvas, but nearer, coming out to meet them, was the schooner-rigged pilot boat. Close enough to hail, she came about and ran alongside.

"What ship is that?" shouted her captain through a speaking trumpet.

"*Javelin*, out of Boston, Captain Sprague commanding," the answer went back.

"Stand by, *Javelin*, to take your pilot aboard," called the schooner's captain, and in a moment a boat was lowered. Sprague and Langdon were at the rail to greet the pilot when he came over the side.

"You've made a fast voyage," said the San Francisco man. "Ninety days, isn't it, since you left Boston? Too bad you were fog-bound. We'd sighted you and were ready to come out. Now I'll take you right in, so you'll be ahead of the other ship out there. Who is she, do you know?"

"Not sure," Captain Sprague replied, "but we think she's the *Goldfinder*—cleared from New York one day ahead of us."

The pilot grinned. "We heard about the race," he said, "by telegraph and pony express. She hasn't been reported yet. I reckon some money'll change hands, now that you're in port."

Smartly, with all sails drawing, the clipper swept through the Golden Gate. Bob stood there open-mouthed, staring at the brown heights of the mountain to the northward. Then all hands were sent aloft to shorten sail. At eleven o'clock that morning, the *Javelin* dropped anchor in the harbor of San Francisco.

VIII

Word of the clipper's extraordinary voyage must have spread fast in the booming port. Almost before the hook was down, two small boats put off from the Embarcadero and raced for the moored ship. In them were rival newspapermen, trying to scoop each other on the story. They arrived together and had to be content with asking their questions in chorus. Of course they wanted to know first whether the *Javelin* and the *Goldfinder* had been within sight of each other all the way. Captain Sprague smiled.

"No," he said, "we had no idea where the other ship was until the day before yesterday. She'll be coming through the Gate almost any time now—if that *is* the *Goldfinder*."

Other questions concerned the weather they had encountered, their best day's run, and what sort of cargo they had brought. In return, the reporters gave a glowing account of new discoveries in the gold fields, the latest prospectors to become millionaires, and the most lurid of the recent murders.

The crew, supposed to be busy about the deck, listened goggle-eyed. Bob could see that many of them were fidgety —hardly able to wait for a chance to get ashore. The fourth mate looked at them pityingly.

"Poor devils!" he said to the boys. "They'll jump ship today or tomorrow an' make tracks for the diggin's. Then, if they don't get killed, we'll see 'em on the beach next time we're in port. Some of 'em may beg to sign on again. Others'll be shanghaied an' have to sweat under tough

bucko mates aboard other ships. Sailors never seem to know when they're well off."

The city, what they could see of it from the clipper, looked raw and new, but there was a bracing air of self-confidence about it. Rows of frame houses climbed the hills. Some were unpainted, but others glowed pink or white or yellow in the sunlight. Down along the water front all was bustle. Drays hauled freight from the docks to long warehouses. Chinese coolies, with pigtails and wide straw hats, trotted back and forth carrying prodigious loads.

There were half a dozen other ships at anchor in the roadstead. Barges and scows were laid alongside to take their cargoes ashore, and by midafternoon a small, puffing steamboat towed a barge out to the *Javelin*.

The ship's officers had laid down the law. No shore leave would be granted till the hold was empty. With that in mind, all hands worked like beavers at the unloading, and before the day's end, nearly half the cargo had gone ashore.

About five o'clock that afternoon a tall, graceful clipper had sailed in and taken her berth less than a cable's length away. Captain Sprague had been ashore most of the afternoon, visiting the firms to whom his cargo was consigned. Hardly had he come back aboard when the skipper of the newly arrived ship hailed the quarterdeck.

"This is Captain Thomas of the *Goldfinder*," he called through a megaphone. "I see you beat us in. Great work! Can you come over for dinner?"

"Congratulations, Captain, on a fine voyage," Sprague replied. "But since we were here first, I think I should have the honor of playing host. Bring any of your mates who won't be on duty. We'll eat at seven."

This was the first state dinner served aboard the *Javelin*, and it had to be done in style. The steward, a fussy little man named Daggett, came hurrying forward to locate Bob and Matt.

78

"Ship's boys have to act as waiters at an affair like this," he told them. "Come with me and get some clean trousers and jackets. Then I'll show you your duties."

Matt wrinkled his nose in distaste as they followed him aft. "Didn't know I'd have to be a servant when I shipped," he whispered in Bob's ear.

The Kittery boy laughed. "I call it a lark," he replied. "We'll get to hear all about the *Goldfinder*'s voyage, and I bet we'll eat a lot better than we would forward."

When they had dressed in their white coats and trousers, the steward looked them over critically. "Too bad you didn't have time to get your hair cut," he said, "but otherwise I guess you look well enough. Here's my comb. Slick your hair down as much as you can. Now, then—you'll bring on the plates, starting with the visiting captain, then our skipper, then the mates, by rank. I'll pour the wine myself. Try not to be as clumsy as I'm afraid you are."

The long table was set in the cabin, with a white cloth, gleaming glass and silver—everything as handsome as possible. The boys practiced handing plates from the left, moving quietly, and standing at attention at opposite sides of the table.

Meanwhile, under the steward's supervision, Absalom had been outdoing himself at his galley stove, and everything was in readiness when the bosun piped the guests over the side. The ship was as clean and trim as the hardworked crew could make it, sails neatly furled and the house flag flying at the peak.

Bob saw Captain Thomas cast a quick, appraising eye aloft. Apparently he could find nothing to criticize, even if he had been unmannerly enough to make a remark. He was a youngish man, red-faced and portly. The first and third mates of the *Goldfinder* accompanied him, both smart-looking fellows in their twenties.

Once the first greetings had been exchanged, the party

went to the cabin for sherry. Then the boys began serving. There was a clear soup to start with, followed by broiled fish, purchased by the steward on shore, roast beef and vegetables, figs and oranges that also came from the water-front markets, and black coffee. Daggett had kept the wineglasses filled during the meal. When the men settled back with their cigars, it was obvious that all had enjoyed their dinner.

There had been some good-natured chaffing among the younger officers about the race, and a complimentary speech by Captain Thomas. Now, while Bob went about clearing the table with as little disturbance as possible, he learned something he hadn't known before.

"Perhaps," Thomas was saying, "we can give you a better test on the voyage home. When do you plan to sail, sir?"

"I've had a change of orders," Sprague replied. "We'll go in ballast to Canton and load with tea for London. So, unless you're westbound, too, I'm afraid we'll have to postpone our next contest."

Bob could hardly wait to get outside and find his chum. They would be sailing around the world! What more could a ship's boy ask on his first voyage?

Matt was less surprised than he expected. "I knew there was a chance of it," he said, "from something I heard Mr. Chase and Dad discussing one night. They say the freight on tea from China's worth going after. A fast clipper can make double the rates they give the old East India ships, because the tea comes into the London market fresh. I sure hope we get a few weeks in port here, though. Wouldn't you like to go up to Sacramento an' see the gold mines?"

Bob admitted he would, though he had no money and would have to draw an advance on his wages. They got their own supper in the galley—leftovers from the officers' banquet—and went to their bunks. Bob found it hard to get to sleep. He missed the constant noise and motion of a ship at sea.

*　　*　　*

Next morning Langdon and Gilman took the prisoner Grogan ashore and had him lodged in jail. When the last of the cargo was out of the hold, half the crew got shore leave. It was the starboard watch that went first, whooping and skylarking as they tumbled into the longboat. Bob and Matt, with the rest of the port watch, looked after them enviously. Sea bags and chests had to be left on board, and the foremast hands had received only a small part of their pay.

George Preble grinned as he saw them go. "Thirty men," he said. "You'd think they'd want their belongings and the money that's coming to 'em. But if we get twenty of 'em back, it'll be a miracle. I noticed some of 'em looked sort of fat around the middle—smuggling what they could off the ship. Not much we can do about it, though. One good thing—it's the riffraff that usually jumps ship and the able hands that stick."

By midnight that night fourteen men had returned, and five more came straggling back next day. All but a handful were suffering from massive hangovers, and more than one showed a black eye.

Matt and Bob had their turn ashore with the second contingent. The two boys wandered back from the docks, climbed Nob Hill to see the view, then came back through Chinatown, peering into dingy little shops and wondering what it was like in the opium dens that were said to lie behind and beneath those ramshackle buildings. In the dusk they saw hundreds of Chinese coming back from work. Their yellow faces were blank, and their hands were folded inside the sleeves of their blue cotton jumpers. In sandals

81

or queer little cloth slippers they moved along in the shadow of the houses at a quick, noiseless shuffle.

The boys had supper in the cleanest small restaurant they could find, and were scandalized at the cost—a whole dollar for steak, potatoes, and pie. Everything in San Francisco seemed to be priced two or three times as high as in New England.

The lights were on now in the dance halls and saloons along Market Street. They strolled past gaudy gambling places, all plush and gilt, and saw bejeweled ladies and their top-hatted escorts leave the hotels to drive off in shining carriages.

"Gosh!" said Matt. "I went to New York once and I thought that was gay, but it can't touch this place!"

Down nearer the water front they came back to the town's seamier side. There the grogshops stood shoulder to shoulder for blocks. Sailors and miners drank under the smoky lights, played poker or faro, sang and argued and fought.

The noise was ear-splitting. Drunken voices mingled with the jangling music of pianos and were punctuated by occasional gunshots. Once they saw a man stumble out of a doorway and pitch headlong into the ankle-deep mud. Thinking he had merely been thrown out of the saloon, they would have walked past, but Bob clutched Matt's arm and halted him.

"Look!" he said, aghast. "A knife in the middle of his back!"

It was true. They bent above the victim and stared in horror at the dirk, buried to the hilt between the shoulder blades. Blood was oozing from the wound. Matt felt the man's pulse and found he was dead. They looked around in vain for a policeman.

"Gosh!" said Bob. "Come to think of it, there aren't any

police. At least I haven't seen one all evening. What can we do?"

"Nothing," Matt answered. "Let's get out o' here. The poor fellow's dead and I guess it isn't any of our business."

Shaken by the experience, they hurried on along the docks till they came to the place where they had landed that afternoon. The longboat had returned to the ship and wouldn't be back till midnight, but they decided they had seen all they wanted of San Francisco. A rat-faced boatman with an unkempt beard sat hunched on the pier. When he saw them standing there, he got up and approached them.

"Take ye out to yer ship for a fiver," he whined.

"You're crazy," Matt told him. "I'll give you a dollar, an' that's more than it's worth."

The fellow shrugged. "I don't have to go no place," said he. "No mate's waitin' fer me with a belayin' pin."

"All right—two dollars," Matt replied. "Take it or leave it."

The man grinned behind his straggling whiskers. "What ship are ye on?" he asked. "If she don't lie too fur out, I'll carry ye fer three dollars."

They finally settled for two dollars and a half and got into the battered skiff that was tied to the wharf. The man rowed out a hundred yards or so and rested on his oars.

"Let's see the color o' yer money," he growled. "Then maybe I'll take ye the rest o' the way."

"A dollar now," said Matt, "and the rest when we get there." He reached into his pocket before Bob could warn him and pulled out the small roll of bills.

"Greenbacks, eh?" sneered the boatman. "Ye're a tenderfoot fer fair! Out here we like silver dollars, or else gold dust."

Nevertheless, his eyes stayed greedily on the bills in

Matt's fist. Stealthily his right hand crept behind him and flashed out holding a foot-long seaman's knife.

Bob, too, had moved quickly. When he got into the skiff, he had seen a boat hook tucked under the after thwart, where he was sitting. Now he jerked it out and held it with the sharp point aimed at the man's breast.

"You get back to your rowing," he said. "Put your money away, Matt."

For a moment the boatman stared at the threatening spike just out of his reach. Then he dropped the knife and picked up the oars again.

"Don't git het up, young feller," he whined, with what was meant to be a disarming smile. "Jest show me where yer ship's moored."

Bob didn't fall for the ruse. He held the boat hook steady and let Matt do the pointing. In five minutes they were at the foot of the rope ladder hanging over the side.

"Deck ahoy!" called Bob and was glad to see the third mate come to the rail.

"Take a good look at this fellow, Mr. Snow," he said. "Better warn the boys to keep away from him. He likes money too much an' he's a lot too handy with a knife."

"Give you any trouble?" asked Snow.

"Not much. I'd have speared him through the gizzard if he had. What's the right price for a boat out to the ship?"

"Generally a dollar," the mate replied. "If you think he's earned it, that is."

Matt left a dollar bill on the thwart and scrambled up the ladder. Bob followed him, still holding the long-handled weapon till he was out of knife range, then letting it clatter down into the skiff. The man below yelled a stream of curses after them, but they noticed he pulled away in some haste.

"Whew!" said Matt. "Some place—this San Francisco!

That's the second time you've saved my money for me, Bob. Maybe this time it was my life!"

For an hour or two the boys sat on the deck, listening to the muffled clamor of the wide-open seaport at night. A little before twelve o'clock the longboat put off, and it returned half an hour later loaded with what was left of the port watch. A few of the men were still hiccuping barroom songs, but most were in a drunken stupor and had to be hoisted aboard.

In the morning the crew was set to painting, always a much-needed job after a long voyage. Bob and Matt were using their brushes on the capstan and other ironwork forward when George Preble came over to them.

"You boys got any plans for the next week or two?" he asked.

Bob shook his head. "We don't care much about more shore leave after what we saw o' the town," he replied.

"Well," said the young fourth mate, "we'll be in port till the week before Christmas, an' I'd like to wangle a trip to the gold country. Don't like to go alone, though. If I can get you the leave, would you two be interested in coming along?"

"You bet!" they told him promptly. "When do we start?"

"Tomorrow, if I can work it out with the skipper. I'll let you know."

IX

Preble kept his word. He not only obtained permission for the three of them to take a two-week leave but arranged for Bob to draw some of his wages. They went ashore early next morning, purchased some camping supplies, and carried them down to the dock, where the paddle-wheel steamer *Sacramento* was making ready to depart.

The trip up the slow-flowing river took a day and a night. More than a hundred passengers crowded the little boat's decks, and a more motley collection of people would be hard to find. A few were weather-tanned old sourdoughs, returning to the diggings after a binge in town. But most of the others were making the trip for the first time. There were roughly dressed laborers, pale young clerks, two or three cold-eyed gamblers in expensive clothes, and half a dozen gaudy-looking dance-hall girls. Among the crowd the boys saw several erstwhile sailors from their own ship, doing their best to keep out of sight.

George Preble spotted them and smiled. "The poor chaps have nothing to fear from me," he said with a shrug. "Let 'em have their attack o' gold fever. When it's out o' their systems, they'll come drifting back. Maybe we'll even give some of 'em another chance."

That first morning they chugged up a wide estuary lined on both sides with tall brown reeds, known by the Spanish name of *tule*. At noon they ate bread and cheese. The steamboat made occasional stops alongshore for wood, and at one of these landings there was a farmer selling grapes

and small, bitter oranges. They bought some of his fruit to eat for dessert.

It grew cold after sundown. They wrapped up in blankets and lay close together for warmth, and all three of them slept well enough. In the morning a low, heavy fog cloaked the river—a *tule* fog, the local people called it. But the pilot seemed to know his business. The *Sacramento* churned on without slackening speed.

To quench their thirst, the passengers dipped up river water from over the side. It was brackish-tasting stuff but at least as palatable as the water aboard the *Javelin* after rounding the Horn.

A little past noon the steamer sounded her whistle and steered in for the bank. There was a landing dock, and behind it a little town of frame buildings and adobe shacks. This was Sacramento. When Preble and the boys went ashore, they found that every second or third building was a saloon and that a good half of the population was drunk.

Crowds hung around the assayers' offices to watch prospectors come in with ore samples. There was always the chance that somebody had made a big strike, and whenever that happened, there would be a general stampede to the new find.

Most of the gold, the newcomers learned, was coming out of the hills thirty or forty miles to the east. On every corner they saw men displaying nuggets or bags of gold dust and offering any stranger who looked as if he had money a chance to buy shares in a "sure thing."

"Let's get us some burros or mules an' get started," Preble suggested. But when they asked about pack animals, they were laughed at. There were horses tied at the hitching racks, but no owner would part with one except at a price far beyond their means. Finally the three friends set off on foot, carrying their bedrolls, plus a pick, shovel, hatchet, pans, and heavy sacks of provisions.

They covered five or six miles before nightfall and made a little open camp a short distance from the trail.

"How are your feet holding out?" Bob asked his chum, as they ate flapjacks beside their little fire.

"It isn't my feet," Matt answered ruefully. "It's my back. Man, is that pack heavy!"

Preble laughed. "They all weigh the same," he told them, "only I'm carrying the pick and shovel besides. You'll get used to it, Matt. Just lean forward and walk sort of springy-kneed. We ought to make a long day of it tomorrow—twenty-five miles, I'd guess—so get some sleep now."

It had been hot enough on the trail, but with darkness the damp and chill returned. Bob curled up in his blanket and listened to the eerie howl of coyotes off in the brush. The sound sent a delicious thrill down his spine. He had wanted to know the feel of the "Wild West," and this was it.

The party got moving again soon after daybreak. They were among rolling foothills now, and frequently the trail led through pine woods. Birds, different from the eastern ones Bob knew, flitted and twittered in the branches overhead. A jack rabbit with great mulelike ears leaped across the path and off into the sagebrush. And once, in open country, they saw a colony of prairie dogs.

"You reckon there'll be grizzly bears up in the hills where we're going?" Matt asked.

"Shouldn't wonder," said Preble with a wink in Bob's direction. "Too bad we didn't bring along a rifle. Still, you've got the hand ax in your pack. We'll count on you to protect us."

Early that afternoon the trail led across the bed of a stream. It was nearly dry, but a trickle of water a couple of yards wide still flowed down the sandy bed.

"Hey—let's do some panning!" Matt suggested. "I bet there's gold in that stream."

"Well," George Preble agreed, "it won't hurt us to rest a spell. Go ahead an' pan. I expect everybody who's passed this way has had a shot at it, but it never does any harm to try."

Matt hurried a short distance upstream and began shoveling sand into the wide, shallow pan. He filled it with water and shook it from side to side, sluicing away the dirt. When only the heaviest material remained in the bottom, he examined it eagerly.

"See any color?" Preble called.

Matt was silent for a minute. Then he answered with an exclamation. "There are some yellow specks!" he cried. "Come an' look!"

Bob left the grinning mate and ran to join the other boy. Peering into the thin layer of gravel that lay in the bottom of Matt's pan, he saw several small fragments that shone with a yellow glint. At once he was as excited as his friend.

"Hey!" he shouted. "He's right—come see for yourself!"

Preble sauntered up and gave the pan a careful examination. "I'd say it's mica, offhand," he commented. "Fool's gold, they call it. Still, o' course I could be wrong."

He picked up some of the specks and tried to weigh them in his hand. "Doggone if I don't believe it *is* gold," he said.

Bob had already seized his own pan and set to work, and in a moment all three of them were frantically washing gravel. Within half an hour they had collected enough of the yellow particles to make a tidy little pile in the middle of George Preble's handkerchief. It was heavy—no question about it. If it really was gold, they must have found thirty or forty dollars' worth.

Then suddenly, as Bob dug into the stream bed with his hands, he came up with an irregular chunk of mineral half an inch across. He could feel the weight of it among the small stones and sand. And when he rubbed away the dirt that clung to it, the nugget gleamed with the true color of gold. For a moment he couldn't talk. Slowly and carefully he carried his treasure to George Preble.

"Look," he said, in a voice that was barely above a whisper. "Is this real?"

The young mate set down his pan and stared at the odd-shaped blob of metal in Bob's palm.

"Let me heft it," he said. "Golly, boy—yes! It's real, right enough. Must weigh a couple of ounces. Hang on to that an' you'll have the handsomest stickpin in New England!"

Matt came over to see it and his eyes fairly popped. "Say!" he breathed. "I've got to get one o' those, too! Why don't we camp right here on this creek? I bet we won't find any better place, however far we go."

They talked it over, and Preble agreed to spend the night there. "We'd better make camp further up, where we'll be out o' sight o' the trail," he said. "A lot o' rough characters travel this way."

Even as he spoke, they heard the clink of hoofs on stony ground, and two men on horseback, leading pack mules, came down the trail from the east. As they reached the ford, they halted to water their animals and looked in the direction of the three farther up the stream. One of them laughed.

"Hey, you greenhorns!" he shouted. "What do ye expect to find? Every tenderfoot in Californy's panned that creek. Ye'll have to travel another forty mile to find any gold!"

Bob stared at the pair, fascinated. They were typical prospectors, heavily bearded, dressed in red plaid shirts, trousers tucked into cowhide boots, and "wide-awake" hats —rakish felts with the brims turned up in front. Each of them wore a cartridge belt strapped low around the hips and a big revolver in a holster prominently displayed. From the thinness of their packs, he judged they were on their way to purchase fresh supplies.

"Thanks," George Preble called back to them. "We're just getting some practice here. Be moving on soon."

The two men laughed again, shook their heads pityingly, and clattered away down the trail. When they were gone, Matt wanted to go back to panning, but Preble looked at the setting sun and decided they should find a camping spot. They carried their gear half a mile farther up the creek and picked a place behind a clump of alders, well out of sight from the trail. Before dark they had gathered dry wood and sagebrush for a small campfire. Sitting around it after they had eaten, they talked over plans for the rest of their leave.

"If we could do as well every day," said the mate, "I wouldn't mind staying right here. What do you say we try it again tomorrow an' see?"

The boys were more than willing. Again they slept under the stars and woke at dawn to start panning once more. On the theory that the gold in the stream bed must have washed down from rich deposits in the hills, they worked farther and farther up, covering several miles before noon. To their disappointment practically nothing but dirt showed up in the pans. And even more discouraging, the higher up the creek they went the more old diggings they found. Hundreds of people before them must have had the same idea, for there were charred ashes from many campfires and scars of picks and shovels everywhere.

That night they returned to the camp back of the alders, and the next morning they tried again at the original location, just above the ford. This time their luck seemed to be out. Several hours of hard work netted them only a few small specks of gold.

"About four bits' worth, I should judge," said Preble ruefully. "We must have got all there was that first day. What do you say we head on east?"

Once more they shouldered the packs and trudged uphill along the trail. The sky had clouded over. By midafternoon it had begun to rain—a steady, mournful, uncomfortable drizzle that wet them to the skin. Bob began to wish they had brought a tent with them, even though it would have meant a heavier load to carry. Sleeping out in this weather would be a miserable experience.

There was an hour or so of daylight left when they met a man on a pinto horse coming down the trail. He pulled up beside them at George Preble's hail.

"Any settlement near here?" asked the mate. "We're looking for a place to sleep."

The rider looked at them with amusement. He was dry enough under a poncho. "Only place close is Birdie's Gulch," he replied. "Ain't exactly a settlement, but I reckon ye kin git under cover. It's in a little canyon, a couple o' miles on ahead."

They thanked him and plowed on through the mud. After nearly an hour's slogging, they stumbled down the path into a narrow gorge and saw two or three buildings beside the trail. A light shone feebly in the largest of them.

Preble knocked on the door, and after a moment it was flung open by a woman—Birdie herself, as they soon found out. She was a brassy-haired blonde of uncertain age and mammoth proportions. She had arms like a blacksmith's and a voice that reminded Bob of a Maine Coast foghorn.

"Could we get shelter for the night, ma'am?" the mate asked politely.

She scowled at them, sizing them up. "Two dollars apiece," she announced. "Ye kin sleep in the loft an' I'll throw in yer breakfast. Pay in advance," she added in an ominous rumble. "Supper's a dollar an' it's ready."

They set down their packs on the dirt floor and looked around at the dimly lit interior. A single lamp burned smokily above the rough bar. Birdie's principal stock in trade seemed to be a dozen jugs of redeye whisky on a shelf back of the bar. There was only one other customer. He was a thin figure in the usual checked shirt, his trousers tucked into his big, muddy boots. He was busy scribbling with a stub of pencil in a dog-eared notebook.

The sodden newcomers shouldered up to the counter and Preble carefully produced the knotted handkerchief that held their gold dust. As always in such places, there was a small pair of gold scales on the bar. Birdie weighed out nine dollars' worth of dust and dumped it in a deerskin bag she wore tied to her ample waist.

"That'll pay fer yer beds an' supper," she growled. "Grub'll be comin' right out."

At the interruption to his thoughts, the other man now looked up, frowning. For the first time they realized that under the dark, curly beard his face was that of a youngster. He couldn't have been much older than the two ship's boys.

"Hi," Bob greeted him with a grin. "Looks as if you got caught in the rain, too."

The young fellow nodded and returned his gaze with some curiosity. "From the way you're dressed," he said, "I'd guess you must be sailors. Am I correct?"

He had a pleasant voice and spoke like a person of education.

"That's right," Bob replied. "We're on leave from the clipper *Javelin*. Matt and I are ship's boys. This is George Preble, our fourth mate."

"The *Javelin*, eh?" their new acquaintance exclaimed. "She came in the day I left town. Fastest voyage since the *Flying Cloud*. I expect you're very proud of her."

"We are that!" Preble told him heartily.

"I'm a printer for a newspaper in San Francisco," the young man said. *"The Golden Era.* But what I really want to do is write. Thought I'd travel up this way for some stories. Most of our California news seems to come either from the port or the gold fields. I've only been out here a year. Raised in New York State. My name's Harte—Bret Harte."

X

The "supper," for which they had already paid, turned out to be boiled beans, piled untidily on tin plates. There was no bread—only a thick, muddy liquid in tin mugs that passed for coffee. The one saving quality of the meal was that it was hot. They ate it because they were cold and hungry.

"All right," Birdie announced truculently when they had finished. "None o' ye look minded to buy a drink, an' it ain't likely anybody else'll be droppin' in, so I'm goin' to douse the light. Better git up to the loft while ye kin still see yer way."

They were picking up their packs to obey her orders when there came a pounding at the door. It burst open to admit three miners—big, rough, bearded men who appeared to be old friends of the owner.

"Wal, Birdie!" one of them shouted. "Blame ef ye ain't a sight fer sore eyes! Purtier'n ever! We're wet enough on the outside but plumb dry inside. Set out a jug!"

"Shore, Lem." She laughed coyly and produced a jug and glasses. "What's new up the gulch?"

Quietly the four young Easterners retired to a corner and sat on their packs. For the next two hours they were treated to songs, jests, and various bits of mining gossip while the fiery liquor flowed and the quartet at the bar got drunk.

"One-eye" Melcher, the newcomers reported, had had

his claim jumped and had shot the low-down varmint that did it.

"Got him clean through the head," said the man called Lem. "Purtiest shot ye ever seed—an' he done it from forty paces."

One of the others told about a big strike on Slippery Creek, and how most of the prospectors in the gulch area lit out overnight to get in on it. Other killings and other discoveries of gold were casually mentioned. And all the while young Harte sat there writing industriously in his notebook.

One of the quartet, a hulking miner with a red bush of whiskers, swung around to stare at them. The liquor had inflamed him and he was obviously spoiling for a fight.

"Hey," he said loudly, "what's he doin'—drawin' pitchers of us?"

"Simmer down, Red," the huge woman bellowed cheerfully. "He's jest a kid. Wandered in here lookin' fer news to put in his paper. Leave him be an' maybe ye'll git yer name in print."

The red-bearded man was somewhat mollified. "Wal," he said, after digesting the information, "we better give him suthin' to write about. Lem, tell him 'bout that big grizzly o' yourn."

Lem looked pleased at the invitation. "Got to wet my whistle 'fore I kin talk good," he said, reaching for the jug. He took a long, gurgling pull and wiped his whiskers with the back of his hand.

"Happened thisaway," he began. "I come out here in 'forty-nine an' headed back in the mountains, whar b'ars was a lot thicker'n folks. I left 'em alone an' they left me alone—mostly. One day, though, I come back to my camp from the diggin's, an' settin' by the door was the biggest durn grizzly b'ar I ever seed. Month before I'd toted in a jug o' 'lasses to sweeten my flapjacks, an' this b'ar had it in her paws—that's right, 'twere a she—a-lickin' at the 'lasses stuck 'round the mouth of it.

" 'Hey!' I yelled out. 'Quit messin' with my grub!' An' shore enough she set the jug down, real keerful, an' looked at me so durn comical I had to laff. That done it. She come amblin' over an' put them great monstrous arms 'round me. Like to skeert me to death, but then I realized all she wanted was to show she sort o' liked me.

"Wal, sir, that was the fall o' the year, an' blamed if that ol' b'ar didn't spend the winter right thar in camp. I got used to havin' her 'round an' she made good company in a lonesome place like that. She never did learn to talk more'n a word or two, but talk wa'n't needed. I'd sing sometimes, in the evenin's, or twang a jew's-harp, an' she'd look real pleased. When I got done, she'd clap her paws together so I'd know she enjoyed it."

He paused for another swig of whisky, and Harte spoke up from his corner.

"That was fine and sociable," he said solemnly. "But I should think she'd have been an expensive guest—eaten you right out of house and home."

Lem looked at him with scorn. "Huh!" he said. "Shows how much you know 'bout grizzlies. Didn't I say it was comin' on winter? B'ars nat'rally hibernate in cold weather an' live on their fat. This un didn't go to sleep, but she didn't eat much of anythin' either. Oh—once in a while a mess o' flapjacks an' 'lasses when I asked her to. But on t'other hand, she brung in a lot more'n she et. Sometimes I'd find a deer's carcass when I come in from work. Sometimes it'd be a sheep or a hog that she'd lugged up from a ranch in the valley.

"I tried to teach her to cook, but she never liked messin' 'round a fire. Mighty good worker, though. I called her Griselda—Zelda fer short. When I'd leave in the mornin', I'd say, 'Zelda, them dirty plates don't look very good, an' the floor's sort o' cluttered.' That's all it took. By night everythin' would be neat an' tidy. I never slep' so warm, neither. She'd curl up thar beside me, all big an' furry, an' it was good as a stove."

Lem shook his head, heaved an alcoholic sigh, and wiped away a tear with his sleeve. "Shore hated to lose that b'ar," he said brokenly.

There was a heavy silence in the room. At last Harte could stand it no longer. "Well," he asked, "what happened?"

The miner gave him a reproachful look. "Ye might say what happened was Spring," he replied. "Spring an' Nater. I was workin' away at the diggin's one day in March, an' a big he-grizzly come bouncin' down out o' the piney woods. I thought he looked at me funny when he went by—sort o' hungry-like—but that was nothin' to me. I jest kep' on swingin' my pick. Come suppertime I went back to camp an' sung out a hello to Griselda. But she didn't come to meet me. When I got to the cabin door, the place was plumb empty. All 'round in front was b'ar tracks—Griselda's an' the other feller's—like they'd been doin' a waltz together. Then they'd gone—jest plain skedaddled."

He gave another gusty sigh. "That wa'n't the worst of it though," he continued. "Mebbe I could fergive her fer cravin' the company of her own kind. What really hurt was that when she skipped out, durned if she didn't take my poke o' dust with her—all the gold I'd dug in a year!"

At that the miners could no longer hold in their mirth. Great bellows of laughter shook the rickety building—Birdie's loudest of all. The three sailors laughed with them, and only young Bret Harte kept a straight face.

"Thank you, Lem," he said, when the noise died down. "That was an interesting account of a most unusual incident. I'll include it in my next letter to the paper. Seems to me, though, you should have reported the theft to the marshal. Stealing a man's dust is a very serious offense. I've heard of people being hung for it. But maybe bears are harder to hang."

The laughter roared out again. "Ye're all right, kid!" said the man called Red. "Come have a drink on that."

"Thanks just the same," Harte replied, "but Miss Birdie sent us to bed once, and I think I'll go now."

The three from the *Javelin* rose with him, picked up their packs, and climbed the ladder to the loft.

"Sleep tight," Birdie called after them. "Don't light no matches up there. There's straw to sleep on an' ye'd set the place afire."

A little light came up from the room below, and they groped around till they found piles of straw. Soon they were all lying down. The noise of the carousers below kept on through the better part of the night, but the drumming of rain over their heads made a soothing sound, and Bob was asleep before he knew it.

The downpour had stopped by morning. They got up stiffly in their still damp clothes and let themselves down the ladder. The three miners lay sprawled on the dirt floor, and Birdie was snoring, her head pillowed on the bar.

"Guess we don't collect on that breakfast she promised," said George Preble. "If it was beans again, I'd just as leave pass it up. Come on—soon's we can find some dry brush, I'll cook you a mess o' flapjacks."

Half a mile up the canyon they came to a patch of greasewood. Even after a rain, it held enough resinous oil to burn well, and they had a hot fire going within a few minutes. Young Harte ate his flapjacks gratefully and washed them down with coffee.

"If you gentlemen don't object," he said, "I'd like to

throw in with you. I find it a bit lonely at times, cruising around by myself."

Preble chuckled. "Sure," he said. "I reckon you're welcome. We'd like you even more if you'd brought a mule along. My young friends here seem to think their packs are pretty heavy."

The four of them crossed a wooded ridge and found themselves in another valley that led on into the higher hills. The white peaks of the high Sierra were plainly visible now—so close they seemed only an hour's walk away. Actually the distance must have been forty or fifty miles. They passed two or three small mining camps during the afternoon and saw hard-working men panning or cradling along a dozen little streams.

Finally they came to a creek bed where there was no evidence of any digging. It meandered down out of a tiny, brush-choked canyon that looked inviting.

"Getting on towards dark," Bob suggested. "What's wrong with camping here? Nobody to bother us. It's miles from any other folks."

There were no objections. While a little daylight still remained, Matt and Harte did a bit of panning and found enough "color" to encourage them. Meanwhile, the two Maine men built the fire and cooked the supper.

When they had eaten, washed the utensils, and were sitting around the fire, Matt addressed their new partner. "Don't suppose you sailed 'round the Horn, like we did," he said. "How'd you come out here, Bret—by wagon train overland?"

"No," said Harte. "Sometimes I wish I had. There are three ways to get to California, and I picked the worst. Took a river boat from Cincinnati to New Orleans, then a steam packet across to the Isthmus. If you ask me, Panama's the lowest-down, nastiest place on earth."

"How do you mean?" asked Bob. "It's only thirty miles wide or so. I should think you'd only have been there a day or two."

Harte gave him a pitying look and shook his head. "First of all," he said, "you land in Colon, along with hundreds of other crazy Americans. It's like a pigsty—nothing much but saloons and mosquitoes and snakes. Human snakes, too. The whole country's crawling with half-breed bandits. If you don't get malaria or yellow fever, you start out in little balsa-wood boats that the natives pole and go up the Chagres River. We were lucky. The boat ahead of us was held up and robbed. Two passengers killed. We got through that part safely and set out afoot for Panama City. I want to tell you it was hot on that jungle trail—just steaming. One man in our party got sunstroke and we had to carry him, taking turns at it. Another was bitten by a bushmaster—great long snake, twice as deadly as any rattler. He died within a quarter of an hour, and we had to leave him for the vultures. When we finally came staggering into Panama, what do you think we found?"

"I can guess," said Preble. "People—scads of 'em."

"That doesn't begin to tell it," Harte answered with feeling. "There were two thousand of them, living in tents or camping in the open, all waiting for a ship to take them to San Francisco. Some had been there for months. There were more sick people than well ones. Every few days there'd be a ship come in, and as many as could bribe their way aboard would jam every inch of space. I had the luck to get a job as cabin boy after two weeks of waiting. It wasn't bad except that I had to keep cleaning up all the time after the seasick passengers. I wasn't as sick as they were, but I can tell you I ate mighty little on the voyage.

"By the time we docked, I weighed about a hundred pounds and could hardly drag my bones to a hotel. I vowed right then I'd never set foot on the deck of a sea-going ship again."

"Plan to stay out here the rest o' your life?" asked Bob.

"Why not? To me, California's the most beautiful country I've ever found. A little rough around the edges right now, I admit. But we'll have real law and order before too long—won't have to depend on the Vigilantes. I like the climate. I like the vigorous young men that are settling here. And the land—it'll grow anything. Once a few of us stop digging for gold and start raising crops, you'll see the high prices come down. Are any of you farmers?"

They shook their heads. "All seafaring men, by birth or inclination," said George Preble.

"Too bad," the young writer replied. "A good farmer could make his fortune in five years, down in the San Joaquin Valley."

"Why don't you try it?" asked Matt, and Harte laughed.

"I'm as bad as you sailors," he said. "Born to be a scribbler, I guess. I'd rather write than be rich. Working for the paper, I get to travel around, and they pay me enough to live on. But reporting isn't what I want to do all my life. There are some great stories to be written some day—about the people in the gold camps and about San Francisco, too. I'd like to be the man to write them."

They listened with respect. "Gee," said Bob at last. "A real author! I never talked to one before. Think you'll write about Lem and the old she-bear?"

"Some day, I hope. That one and a lot of others. These people have their own kind of humor, and their own tragedies. Such stories can't be told in dressed-up language. They've got to be in real mining-camp talk if they're going to sound true. That's one thing I'm learning out here—how miners talk. I'd have to leave out the fancy cuss words, of course. Maybe city readers aren't ready for that kind of writing yet, but I'm going to try."

Half an hour later they were in their blankets. For some reason Bob slept uneasily. He was dreaming about grizzlies, and the dream was so real that he woke up with a start. He opened his eyes. There, right above him was an animal—a big animal—standing ghostly gray in the moonlight.

XI

Bob sat up with a choking gasp. For the first time he wished he was armed. The heavy Colt that Preble kept tucked in his waistband or even Matt's hatchet would have been a comfort. Then, as his eyes cleared, he realized that the creature beside him had long ears and hoofs. It wasn't a bear at all but a donkey! He shooed it away a few yards, then lay down and went to sleep again.

At daylight Preble's shout roused them all from their slumber. "Look here!" he called. "We've got company!"

The rough-coated gray burro stood there, docile and friendly. It looked at them, sleepy-eyed, and switched its little tail. Then it put its ears back and gave forth a bray that would have wakened the dead.

Matt, still more than half asleep, rolled out of his blanket in comical dismay. "Wha—what was that?" he yelped. "For gosh sakes! It's a mule!"

George Preble had approached the beast and was looking it over. "No sign of a halter," he said. "Not even a rope gall. Whoever he belonged to, he hasn't done any work lately. Must have just wandered in here because he likes folks."

Bret Harte chuckled. "In case you're speculating on using him to carry your packs," he remarked, "I'd better warn you. Horse thieves don't get much sympathy around here. If his owner sees you with him, he's likely to shoot first and ask questions afterward."

"I was thinking the same thing," Preble nodded. "I guess

we'll just have to ignore him an' hope he goes away. Too bad, though. He'd make a dandy pack animal."

"Well," said Bob practically, "it's sunup. Time we were panning gold. How 'bout some breakfast?"

They worked over the creek bed with fair success that morning. Amongst them they added a couple of ounces of dust to their collection. Then, trying a little farther up the canyon, behind a clump of brush, Bob came on a sand bar that looked more promising. He scooped a few handfuls into the pan, filled it with water, and started shaking. As the dirt sluiced off, he looked at the residue in the bottom of the pan and was struck speechless. Instead of the usual two or three specks of gold, there were hundreds of tiny yellow-gray flecks, and the pan felt heavy in his hands.

Hastily he stumbled back to his companions. He was on first-name terms with the mate now. "George," he said, "unless I'm seeing things, this is the richest find yet. Look and tell me what you think."

Preble took the pan to the water and gave it a second careful washing. When he looked up, his face was alight.

"Come on, boy," he panted. "Show us where you got it. There's two ounces right here in this one pan. Forty dollars' worth o' dust!"

They attacked the sand bar in a kind of frenzy. Few pans came up with as much gold as the first one, but it was by all odds the richest find they had made. Before noon they had collected nearly thirty ounces—a hundred and fifty dollars apiece after it was split four ways. Then suddenly the gold ran out. Pan after pan showed nothing but sand and gravel without a single flash of color.

"Pockets are like that, I'm told," said Harte. "Some freak of current washes a lot of gold into one spot. There may not be much of it, and no amount of hunting shows where it came from."

Nevertheless, they went on up the canyon, hopefully

searching for another bar or pocket. At sundown they gave up in disgust, their visions of great wealth shattered.

"Well, our long-eared friend seems to have gone, anyhow," Bob observed as they ate supper. "Hope he went back to the fellow that owns him. Where'll we head tomorrow?"

"Our leave's almost half gone," George Preble reminded him. "Got to start back soon, but we don't have to go home the same way. I figured we might strike south. Angels' Camp can't be much more'n thirty miles, an' I've heard it's fairly quick from there back to the Bay."

"I'll go with you part of the way," said Harte. "I'm not ready to head back to San Francisco yet, but I'd like to see the Tuolumne country, and the mountains up by Yosemite."

In the early dawn they packed up and started southward through rough, hilly country. By ten o'clock they had covered some eight miles—"mostly up an' down," as Matt complained. They sat down to rest on a fallen log and heard something coming through the brush behind them. Then the loud bray of the burro told them they had been followed. He sauntered out into the open, looking sleepy as always but obviously glad to see them.

"All right," said Preble with a grin, "I'm sick o' this foolishness. The jackass has adopted us, an' he might as well share the work along with the fun. Come here, Jack!"

The burro looked bored and put down his head to pull a bit of grass.

"He doesn't know himself by a Yankee name," said Harte. "This fellow's a real Californio. Here, Pedro, *amigo!*"

At once the animal pricked up his ears and came ambling nearer. Within minutes they had loaded the packs on his back. None of them knew how to throw a diamond hitch, but they made the load fast with bits and pieces of rope, the knots tied sailor-fashion. Then they set off again, urging the burro on with a stick. They made better time now. Though the sure-footed beast never seemed to hurry, he moved as fast as they wanted to go.

They crossed several creeks during the afternoon, all of them low enough to ford without swimming. And just as darkness fell, they came in sight of Angels' Camp below them in a canyon.

"Better leave Pedro up here," said Preble. "Somebody down in town might recognize him an' start shooting."

They tethered the burro to a tree and lugged their packs down the hillside. There were two so-called hotels in the camp, and though the prices were high, they got tolerable beds and decent suppers. In the morning Preble inquired about the trail westward.

"Best bet," replied the hotel barkeep, "is to take a boat down the Stanislaus River. They run every day or two, an' if there's enough water, they take ye down pretty fast. The landin' ain't but four or five mile from here."

It was with genuine regret that they parted from young Bret Harte. He had been good company and had done his share of the work without complaining.

"I reckon old Pedro's all yours now," Bob told him. "No good to us on a boat, but you can sure use him over those mountains. Maybe you'll be back in Frisco before we sail. Anyhow, we'll be watching for some o' those stories when they come out."

They hiked five miles down the canyon to the riverbank and sat down to wait. Late that afternoon a big bateau, poled by two boatmen, pulled in to the landing from down-river. A dozen prospectors and tenderfeet piled out, paid their fares, and set off for the little mining town. The boat-men said they would be starting back at daybreak and named a price of a hundred dollars for the three of them.

"Sounds high, but we'll be waiting for you," said Preble. "Hope you're sober when you come back."

The bearded steersman scowled, then decided to take the remark as a joke. "Drunk or sober," he replied in a thick brogue, "Paddy Mulligan'll git ye to the Bay."

He was as good as his word. Red-eyed and reeking of liquor, he and his partner returned to the landing at six in the morning. From the looks of them they hadn't been to bed at all, but they shoved off promptly and steered the rushing current without mishap. Once, at some steep rapids, the passengers had to get out and help carry the boat around. But she flew through other stretches of white water like a bird. They covered close to eighty miles in twelve hours and by dark were well below the place where the Stanislaus joined the San Joaquin.

There was a landing there, at a place called Lundy's Bend. They pulled in beside the crude pier and were immediately surrounded by a swarm of gold seekers asking about transportation up the river. The place was full of them—mostly greenhorns who had come up by steamboat through San Pablo and Suisun Bays. Preble and the boys unloaded their packs. The San Francisco boat wouldn't arrive till noon the next day, so it would be necessary to spend the night there.

None of the lodging houses had even one bed to spare. However, the weather looked as if it would stay clear, and they were now well accustomed to sleeping on the ground. Up on a knoll, a quarter mile above the landing, they found a camp site of sorts and cooked their supper.

"Supplies have about run out," the young mate reported. "Guess we'll have just enough left for our breakfast, come morning."

Fortunately, they were far enough out of town so that the drunken uproar didn't keep them awake. Even the occasional gunshots roused them only momentarily. It was a much smaller sound that woke Bob about two o'clock. In fact, it was hardly a sound at all, though when he thought about it afterward, it seemed as if he had heard breathing.

He opened his eyes and lay perfectly still. A figure was moving stealthily in the darkness only a few feet away. It was a man, crouching low. He stooped over Matt's blanket and for a second Bob saw the glint of a long-bladed knife in his hand.

Bob got his feet under him without making a sound. He had no weapon, but he knew he must act fast. "George!" he yelled, and at the same instant he launched himself at the bent back.

His opponent was big, strong, and wiry, but the boy had the advantage of surprise. He struck hard, catching the intruder off balance and throwing him forward on his face. The knife was still clutched in his right fist, and Bob reached out both hands to grab for it. Then, as the man twisted from under him, he found himself on the bottom, still clinging desperately to the wrist of the hand that held the knife.

His grip was slipping as the man wrenched his arm back and forth. But at that moment Preble came charging into the fray. He caught the unknown enemy by the back of the neck and jerked him half upright, then sent a fist crashing into his face. As the man fell, he dropped the knife and the mate kicked it away. Two more blows, one to the stomach and one to the jaw, finished the fight.

Preble lighted a match and held it a foot from the unconscious man's face.

"Well, by thunder!" he panted. "If it isn't that scurvy Grogan! Must ha' busted out o' the calaboose!"

Bob was on his feet again and Matt was finally awake. They stared at the bearded face till the match went out.

"What happened?" asked Matt in a daze. "Where'd he come from?"

"He was about ready to stick that knife in your gizzard," the mate told him. "Good thing Bob tackled him in time an' woke me up. He had it in for you boys ever since you found his nest in the hold. I reckon he spotted us last night an' came up here to get even."

"What are we going to do with him?" Bob asked. "I don't suppose there's any kind o' law in a place like this."

"No," said Preble. "Guess not. About all we can do is tie him up good an' tight an' go back to sleep."

They made a thorough job of lashing Grogan's arms behind him and tying his ankles to his wrists. Bob took the knife and put it under the pack he used for a pillow. He didn't know whether he could sleep or not, but at least he would have a weapon handy if the man managed to pull free of his bonds.

Actually he did doze off, waking to hear their captive groaning and thrashing about on the ground. He was still there when daylight came, and they went cheerfully about getting their breakfast while he strained at the cords, cursing them with every breath.

Preble turned him over with his boot to make sure the knots still held. "I'm going to leave you right where you lie," he said. "Should have shot you out o' hand last night for the murdering robber you are. But I won't do it now in cold blood. We'll be gone by the time anybody finds you, an' I guess it won't be too much punishment to let you stay here with no food an' nothing to drink. If you ever cross my path again, I warn you, I aim to kill you on sight."

With that final admonition the three of them shouldered their packs and went down to the landing. When the little steamboat came in and discharged its passengers, they were surprised to see another familiar face. It was the steward, Daggett. He was superintending the unloading of a lot of freight—crates and barrels of food.

Preble faced him. "Well," he said, "you must be planning on quite an expedition."

The little man looked up, startled, then assumed a defiant air. "I'm done with the ship," he replied. "Aim to make some money while it's still plentiful. I'm startin' an eatin' place here at Lundy's Bend."

Preble laughed. "Good luck," he said. "When you're settled, today or tomorrow, you might mosey up to the knoll over yonder. We left a friend o' yours there. Time you find him, he'll likely be good an' hungry for some o' your vittles."

The steamer paused only to take on water and firewood, then puffed out into the river channel. By six o'clock that evening they docked at San Francisco, and another half hour found them back aboard the *Javelin*.

Captain Sprague gave them an ironic greeting. "S'pose you're all rich now," he remarked. "Think you've had enough o' the gold fields?"

While Absalom was rustling up supper for them, George Preble gave the skipper a brief account of their adventures.

"Ran into Grogan, up on the San Joaquin," he said. "Sort o' surprised us, for we thought he was still in jail. Had to beat him up a little or he'd have done some cutting an' robbing."

The captain frowned. "I hadn't heard he was loose," he replied. "Probably bribed a guard or just broke his way out. Their jail here's a joke."

"One more thing, sir," the mate told him. "I don't know whether you know it, but we're short a steward."

"You mean Daggett jumped ship?" asked Sprague in angry surprise. "I gave him money to provision the ship day before yesterday. Thought he was one man I could trust. Where'd you see him?"

"Lundy's Bend," said Preble. "He bought the provisions,

right enough, but he's using 'em to start a restaurant for himself. After seeing us, he probably went on somewhere up-river, where he'll be out o' reach."

The captain stamped up and down the afterdeck. "Confound it!" he growled. "This gold fever turns even honest men into rascals! We can pick up a crew o' sorts, but where'll we find a steward? I'm about ready to sail."

"You want me to go ashore an' hunt for one, sir?" asked Preble.

"No. The other mates are on leave. You take charge o' the harbor watch an' I'll go myself."

He took off with two men in one of the small boats a few minutes later, and Preble and the boys were left to watch the deck. Darkness had shut down and a thin fog obscured the shore. From the direction of the water front the sounds of revelry and quarreling came with extra loudness through the mist.

Bob stood by the rail in the waist, staring into the curtain of fog and listening to the noises, eerily close. Suddenly he heard drunken voices that seemed to come from right abeam.

"Thar he goes!" . . . "Kill the yaller devil!" . . . "Smash him, Bill!" . . . "Gun him down!"

There was a sound of feet pounding along a dock and the loud blast of a gun. Then silence shut down except for the gurgle and lap of water around the hull.

XII

In the next ten minutes Bob had almost forgotten the incident. Chasing Chinese was a sport enjoyed by the riffraff of the docks, he knew. It was like hunting rabbits, for the poor coolies never fought back, and he had heard it said that "nobody ever went to jail for killing a Chinaman."

He was thinking about his share of the gold dust and what he would do with it when another sound reached his ears—a splashing in the water just below him. Then he heard a choking cry. Looking down, he caught a glimpse of a pale blob that must be a face.

"Hey, Matt!" yelled Bob. He seized the nearest coil of rope and dropped the loose end over the rail. The face in the water had disappeared for a moment. Now he saw it again and, beside it, a feebly moving arm.

"Hang on to this line," he told Matt. "Somebody's drowning down there."

With that he went over the side and down the rope like a monkey. By good luck his bare toes touched the swimmer's body as he went into the water. Quickly he grabbed for the man's arm and pulled his head above the surface.

"He's all in," Bob called to his friend on deck. "Too far gone to hold the rope. I've got to tie it around him."

He made fast a loop of the line under the man's arms. Then he swarmed up it himself, and together he and Matt hauled the limp weight to the deck. They knelt over the thin body, squeezing the ribs to force out the salt water.

"For heaven's sakes!" said the Boston boy. "Look at him —a Chinaman!"

Bob nodded. "I heard 'em trying to catch him on the dock. Never thought he'd swim this far, though. Let's keep trying—I think he's coming to."

By the time the half-drowned man was breathing wheezily again, Preble had joined them.

"Where'd he come from?" he asked. "An' what's his name?"

The Chinese opened his eyes and looked up imploringly. "Name Wing Lee," he managed to whisper. "No go back shoreside, please. Plenty bad men wanting kill me."

"You mean you swam all the way to the ship?" the mate asked in amazement. "Never heard of a Chinaman that could swim like that."

Wing Lee nodded and tried to smile. "Me glow up 'long Canton," he explained. "Live on sampan. Allee time swim."

As his fear subsided and his breath came back, he told them more about himself. He had had some education, it seemed, and had wanted to see the world. Brought over with a shipload of coolies two years before, he had worked first in a laundry, then gone to one of the hotels as a kitchen boy.

"Me plenty good cook," he said proudly. "Make Chinese food taste velly fine."

On this unlucky night he had been sent out to buy vegetables. On his way back, carrying a heavy sack of onions and potatoes, he had been set upon by some drunken longshoremen. He could, he said, have dropped the bag and run away, but the vegetables belonged to his employer and he tried to defend them. The next thing he knew a crowd had gathered and somebody knocked him down. He was beaten and kicked. When they said they were going to kill him, he broke away and ran down the wharf with guns shooting behind him. Swimming blindly, the *Javelin* was the first ship he reached.

George Preble rubbed his jaw reflectively. "Don't rightly know what to do with you," he said. "It's a fact they'd probably murder you if we took you back now. But what you could do to be useful aboard here is more'n I can see. We're sailing for China in a couple o' days."

Wing Lee fell on his knees before the mate. "You go China-side? Mebbe-so you take me 'long?" he pleaded. "No money but can work plenty. Cook—wait on table—wash dishes—wash clothes!"

Bob, who had saved the poor fellow's life, felt responsible for him. "If he can do all those things," he said, "why wouldn't he fit into the steward's job? I mean it. I bet he'd take better care o' you in the cabin than old Daggett ever did."

"Well," Preble replied doubtfully, "the skipper's likely got himself a steward by now. Besides, all we know about Wing Lee is his own say-so. Still, it might work out at that."

An hour later they heard the creak of oars, and Captain Sprague's boat pulled alongside. Nobody was with him but the two men who had rowed him ashore, and his face, in the light of the lantern, was gloomy. Preble went aft with him. In a few minutes the mate returned and beckoned to the young Chinese.

"Come on, Wing Lee," he said gruffly. "Cap'n wants to talk to you."

Bob gave his protégé a pat on the back. "Good luck!" he murmured, and the slim, damp figure padded off in the wake of the mate.

At midnight the longboat brought the officers and men who had been on shore leave back aboard. Bob and Matt turned in while the others took over the harbor watch. It wasn't until they came on deck next morning that they learned Wing Lee had been signed on.

"It's just on sort of a trial basis," Preble told them. "The skipper had his doubts, but after the breakfast Wing cooked and served us this morning, I reckon he'll do all right. I'm going ashore with him later on and help him pick up supplies."

Bob went aft to the steward's pantry and found the young Chinese hard at work. He had washed the dishes, tidied up the cabin, and was busy polishing silver. He greeted the Maine boy with a grin of delight.

"You save life las' night," he said quietly. "Wing Lee never forget. Mebbe some time do favor for you."

"Don't worry about that," Bob laughed. "I knew you were in trouble an' I naturally had to help. Just do a good job here an' we'll get you home to China."

As he was turning away, the young man laid a timid hand on his arm. "You know 'bout fur?" he asked surprisingly. "Rich mans, China-side, give plenty money for fur. Ship can get um cheap up 'long there." He pointed northward.

Bob tried to humor him. "You mean up Oregon way? Or Alaska? What kind o' fur—beaver? Sealskin?"

Wing Lee shook his head. "Sea otter," he said. "One skin, thousan' dollar. Injuns sell cheap."

Bob grinned and went forward again, but the suggestion stuck in his mind. Sea otter. He had heard the animals mentioned somewhere before. Fur so soft and rich there was nothing else like it in the world. That noon he found George Preble and asked if he knew when they would be sailing.

"Day after tomorrow, I reckon, if we can get provisioned an' watered. The ballast's been stowed already, an' I guess we can fill out our crew. Why? You anxious to get ashore again?"

"No," Bob told him, embarrassed. "But I was wondering what Captain Sprague would think o' heading north."

He blurted out Wing Lee's idea about the furs, and Preble listened attentively.

"If there's money in it," he said, "the skipper might take an interest. Wouldn't hurt to ask him. An' while I'm ashore with Wing Lee this afternoon, I'll have a word with him —see if he knows any more'n he told you."

Bob had had little contact with Captain Sprague since they left Boston. In the ordinary routine of the ship at sea, boys weren't supposed to be seen aft except on such duties as reading the log or steering. But in port, discipline was relaxed somewhat. Screwing up his courage, the youngster tiptoed into the officers' quarters and tapped timidly at the captain's door. Bidden to come in, he found the grizzled skipper working on the ship's accounts.

"Yes, Wingate," he growled. "What is it?"

Hesitantly at first, then gaining confidence as he went on, Bob outlined the plan for adding profit to the voyage. "It shouldn't be more'n a week out of our way," he said, "an' according to Maury's Charts we'd have a fair wind an' current all the way from the Northwest Coast to the Sandwich Islands. If you'd let me, sir, I'd like to invest in the venture. My share o' the gold we found is around a hundred an' fifty dollars. I thought I could put some of it into trade goods—beads an' knives an' such—an' buy furs from the Indians. Wing Lee claims the rich Chinese mandarins'll give mighty good money for sea otter skins."

Captain Sprague had listened skeptically. Now he half closed his eyes and thought for a few moments.

"Hmm," he said. "Might be worth a try. I've no way to get word to the owners, o' course, but I'm pretty sure they'd approve. They like fresh ideas for making money. I'll talk to Mr. Langdon about it. He was on that coast as a sealer, years ago. If he thinks the waters aren't too dangerous, we may consider it.

"And thanks, Wingate. I like your ambition." He unbent

enough to give the boy a grin. "If we try it, I'll let you in for a share."

* * *

The *Javelin* put out from San Francisco with the morning tide on the twenty-second of December. She stood well out to sea, heeled far over to the fresh southwest breeze, for she was in ballast now, not deep-laden as she had been on the voyage from Boston.

She was provisioned with the usual casks of beef, pork, and hardtack and carried enough fresh vegetables, they hoped, to last till she reached the mid-Pacific islands. The water tank was filled. A large supply of trade goods, including three barrels of rum, were stored aft for barter with the Indians up the coast.

A crew of sorts had been assembled. About half the original foremast hands had stayed with the ship, and two or three other good seamen, disillusioned by the search for gold, had signed on for the chance of getting home. Finally the crimps had delivered a boatload of drunks and offscourings from the docks the night before she sailed.

Most of the newcomers were violently sick for the first twenty-four hours. After that the mates undertook to knock them into shape and make them useful members of the crew.

Bob had taken Matt into his confidence about the purpose of this northward voyage. Doubtful at first, the Boston boy was now as enthusiastic as Bob could ask, and had invested part of his own gold dust with the skipper.

One of the new men in their watch was a rat-faced limey from the London docks who went by the name of Scully. He was small and wiry and had a high, whiny voice. Bob didn't like him but had to admit he was a first-class seaman —quick as a monkey aloft.

Most of the crew were indifferent to the ship's course. But Scully watched the direction of the sun and the slant of the yards and drew his own conclusions. The third night out he sidled up to Bob and grew confidential.

"Lookee, myte," he said, "'course it ayn't my affair, but I 'eard we was China-bound an' then on to Lunnon. Wot's all this northin' we're mykin'?"

Bob tried to be casual. "Oh, I guess the skipper wants to make a landing some place up the Northwest Coast. We'll be heading for China after that all right."

"Ah," said Scully with a sly nod. "Tradin' with the Hinjuns, I don't doubt. I was there meself in 'forty-eight, 'board of an 'Udson's Bye Comp'ny ship. Learned to talk a bit o' the Hinjun lingo, I did. Might come in 'andy, eh, wot?"

"Might," said Bob curtly and turned away. It was the end of the second dog watch and cold on the deck. As he entered the forecastle, he heard singing—a kind of singing that gave him a twinge of homesickness. Suddenly he remembered that this was Christmas Eve.

There were some fair voices in the crew. They sang carols like "O Little Town of Bethlehem" and "It Came Upon a Midnight Clear," as Bob and Matt joined in. Then some of the Britishers struck up "God Rest Ye Merry, Gentlemen." And a young German with an accordion played and sang "Stille Nacht" and "Tannenbaum."

By Christmas morning they were somewhere off the mouth of the Columbia River, driving along in fog and rain. There was no turkey for the crew that day, but Absalom did his best to celebrate by making what he called plum duff. It was a sort of soggy dumpling with raisins in it and a sweet sauce flavored with a little rum. The foremast hands smacked their lips and proclaimed it the best grub they had tasted in months.

Next day the weather cleared. A sextant shot at noon

showed they were well to the westward of the treacherous Strait of Juan de Fuca. Bob helped the first officer take the reading.

"One more day o' fair wind should do it," said Langdon. "The north end o' Vancouver Island ought to be a good spot for trading. We put in there once, when I was a youngster before the mast. If I recollect right, the Injuns belong to the Haida tribe. We saw a few of 'em. Pretty heathen lot, an' the only way we could talk to 'em was sign language. They did have some sea otter skins, but all we wanted was seal, so we didn't do any trading."

"That new man, Scully, claims he can speak their language," said Bob. "Anyhow, that's what he told me."

"So? Then maybe he'd better be in the boat when we go ashore. Doubt if he'll be much help, though. He looks like a liar to me."

They made a landfall the following morning—a high, rocky coast, shaggy with dark fir forests. By afternoon they had cautiously rounded Cape Scott and come to anchor in Queen Charlotte Sound. The charts were vague, and Captain Sprague decided to keep the *Javelin* well off shore, where he knew there was plenty of water.

A mile and a half away they could see bonfires on the beach as they stood their watches that night. Bob felt a mounting excitement. It was largely through his own efforts that the clipper had come to these little-known waters. And tomorrow he hoped to stand on that wild shore among savages few white men had ever seen before.

XIII

When the longboat was launched next morning, half the crew wanted to go ashore in her. Eighteen men had been picked, and to Bob's delight he was one of them. First Mate Langdon was in command of the party, with Snow acting as his lieutenant. Matt, to his bitter disappointment, was kept aboard the ship.

At the last minute Captain Sprague broke out half a dozen cutlasses for the most dependable members of the boat crew. The two officers were armed with Colts, and Bob was given a big old single-shot naval pistol. He made certain it was loaded and the percussion cap was in place under the hammer before he stuck it in his belt. The weapon, he knew, was good for little but show. However, it gave him a more comfortable feeling.

Ten good men were at the oars as they moved across the blue water toward shore. The breeze was light and off the land, so there was little sea to contend with. Bob and the others who weren't rowing guarded the cases of trade goods and a barrel of New England rum.

"Listen," said Scully when they were still nearly a mile from the beach. "You 'ear wot I 'ear? Drums. They're 'oldin' wot they call a potlatch."

Faintly over the water came the rhythmic boom of a deep-toned drum, and Bob could see a curl of blue smoke rising against the dark background of the forest.

Even as he watched, a long, slim craft shot out from the beach and paddles flashed along its sides. The canoe came out within fifty yards of the longboat, then turned and moved parallel to their course.

"Give way there, hearties!" Langdon ordered. "Show 'em some speed!"

But though the rowers put their backs in it, the Indians easily drew ahead. From that distance the canoe seemed to be hollowed out of a single great cedar log. It was painted a faded red, with a design of blue along the gunwale, and at its bow was the carved head of an animal—a bear, Bob thought.

"Hah!" Scully laughed derisively. "No longboat can catch a Hinjun canoe!"

"What's that thing you were talking about—a 'potlatch'?" Bob asked.

"The 'ole tribe gets together an' 'as a feast an' a big time," the Cockney explained. "W'en they seen the ship come in last night, they sent word for all 'ands to gather 'round—ready fer a fight or a frolic."

"Let's hope it's a frolic," Bob said, laughing, "and that they've got furs to trade."

It wasn't until they came close to the beach that the boy realized the enormous size of the trees. The trunks were six or eight feet through and the tops soared skyward two hundred feet or more, dwarfing the figures of the Indians who waited on the steep, gravelly shingle.

"There's a village 'ere," Scully announced. "A big un, too. See that tall thing with the carved fyces on it? That there's a totem pole."

The canoe reached shore well ahead of them and was quickly pulled up above the tide line. The white rowers rested on their oars a few yards from the beach while Langdon reconnoitered.

"Hello!" he shouted and held up both hands, empty, above his head in a gesture of peace. The Indians—fifty or sixty warriors, naked except for loin cloths—stood like

statues. They were silent, but the drum kept on beating, louder and faster now, in the shadow of the woods. Finally a heavily-built, copper-skinned man in a great feather head-dress took a stride forward.

"That's their chief," Scully whispered. " 'E'll talk."

In a high, singsong voice, the chief began to make a speech.

"What's he say, Scully?" asked the first mate. "Can you figure it out?"

The Londoner waited a moment, hand cupped to his ear. " 'E says if we come peaceable, to tryde, 'e'll let us ashore."

"Well, tell him it's all right. We've got lots of gifts for him."

Scully stood up and mouthed a few phrases of Indian talk, gesturing toward the rum barrel, and immediately the faces of the braves broke into grins. They shouted, capered, and waved their bows and spears.

"What's all that mean?" asked Langdon suspiciously.

"We're welcome," said Scully. " 'Twas the rum done it."

The rowers drove the bow up on the shingle, and Langdon ordered the trade goods put ashore. In a few moments all the men were on land except two, left to guard the boat. They carried the knives and beads, the trade blankets and the rum barrel, up to within a few yards of the chief.

"Now," said the first officer, "tell him we're after furs."

Scully stepped forward and began jabbering again, using his hands in sign talk as well. The chief heard him out, then rubbed his big belly and pointed at the rum barrel.

" 'E clymes 'e can tryde better w'en 'e's 'ad a drink," the limey translated.

"No," Langdon told him firmly. "Tell him we'll open up the rum after we've seen the furs."

This news, passed on by Scully, brought a scowl to the chief's painted face. He talked to some of the other Indians, then dispatched three or four of them back into the woods. They came back with their arms full of pelts—fox and seal and one huge brown bearskin. Meanwhile, the others had drawn closer and were eagerly fingering the trade goods.

"Keep 'em clear," Langdon told the third mate. "I'll take a look at the fur. Come along, Scully."

Under Snow's direction the men from the ship formed a tight ring about the pile of goods. There were some threatening gestures by the braves, but the seamen stood firm. After twenty minutes of haggling, Langdon finally returned and told them to open the barrel. At once it was surrounded by grinning savages holding out bowls made of wood or clay. The chief had the largest one of all, and he held it in both hands, swilling down gulp after gulp of the fiery liquor.

"Hold on, now," said Langdon. "Put the stopper back in the bung. We've got to get some trading done before they're all drunk!"

With Bob assisting him he counted out trade goods—one knife or twenty colored beads for each black fox pelt, a blanket or both knife and beads for a good sealskin. The great bear pelt was too bulky to be worth the price asked. When the furs had been set aside and the goods handed over in trade, the mate called Scully.

That individual had made himself at home with the chief and was eating a steaming dish of clams and fish. It was served on a slab of wood and eaten Indian style, with the fingers. He sauntered over and informed Langdon that the Haida had some sea otter fur but wouldn't produce it until more rum was brought from the ship.

The mate frowned. "How'd he find out we had more?" he asked. "Seems to me you're getting mighty thick with him. All right. Have 'em bring the skins down here, so we can see how many they've got. Tell the chief I'll send for the rum."

Ten minutes later some fifty beautiful silvery gray pelts were produced. After Langdon looked at them he beckoned to Snow. "Take enough men to row," he told him, "an' go get the other two barrels o' firewater. You can carry this first pile o' fur back with you. Don't waste any time. If you hear any firing, bring more men an' guns. Some o' these bucks are starting to get ugly, what with the rum they've already had. An' here—give your revolver to young Wingate."

Bob took the heavy Colt and handed his own weapon to one of the foremast hands. He had felt some of the same apprehension as the first officer.

The boat pulled away, and the dozen of them left on shore stood close to the half-empty barrel watching the cavorting redskins. Bob kept an uneasy eye on Scully, who was now in earnest conversation with the chief. There was something about the Cockney he didn't trust.

Soon the savages began coming back for more rum. Langdon stood by the bung, limiting the amount allowed each brave in spite of their angry jabbering. Bob glanced back at Scully in time to see him make a suspicious motion. He and the chief had their heads together and both were looking at the mate. As if to illustrate what he was saying, the Englishman drew a forefinger quickly across his throat.

Bob moved nearer Langdon. "Better hold it, sir," he said. "I think maybe there's trouble coming."

The mate heard him, knocked the stopper back into the bung, and straightened up. Even as he turned to look, a feathered arrow sang through the air and drove into his chest.

Bob spun, pulling the Colt from his waistband. Hastily he jerked back the hammer. Scully and the chief were running toward them down the beach, each brandishing a spear, and the boy took aim at the white traitor first. The big gun roared, kicking so hard it numbed his hand, but the bullet went true. It knocked the charging Scully backward, a great red hole in his throat.

"Hold 'em off!" Bob yelled at the astonished sailors. "They're trying to kill us all!"

The fat chief, howling his war cry, was only a few strides away. Before he could hurl his spear, Bob fired again, and at the crashing report the Indian sprawled forward on his face.

A score of painted, screaming savages had followed him in the charge. It might have gone hard with the seamen, still confused and disorganized, for the first wave of attackers was almost on them when the chief fell. But that, and the roar of the gun, took all the fight out of the Indians. As suddenly as they had come, they turned and fled back to the shelter of the woods.

"Come on! After 'em!" shouted Bob, and two or three men followed him.

It was probably a foolish move, for once they were hidden by the trees the Indians began to use their bows and arrows. Luckily no one was hit. With his companions the boy grabbed up the sea otter skins and ran back to the little group by the rum barrel. Fifty yards away along the beach there was a big heap of driftwood.

"Everybody over there," Bob panted. "We've got to have cover. You, Dan, give me a hand with Mr. Langdon."

The sailor he addressed helped him lift the wounded mate, and they scrambled after the others. Just as they reached shelter, an arrow grazed Bob's shoulder, tearing his shirt and nicking the flesh. Then they were behind the waist-high barricade of tangled logs and branches.

At once the boy knelt over Langdon. The arrow, he could see, had missed the heart, but the mate was breathing with painful effort and losing a lot of blood. Bob didn't dare to pull the shaft out. For the moment the best he could do was try to stop some of the bleeding.

Ripping his own shirt into long strips and binding them tightly around Langdon's chest, he sent up a silent prayer that the boat would hurry back.

Occasionally there came a blood-curdling yell from the savages in the woods. Arrows continued to fly overhead or plunge viciously into the logs. But terror of the thunder-weapon that had slain their leader kept the Indians from a hand-to-hand attack.

The minutes dragged by endlessly. Watching the ship, Bob finally saw a flash of oars as the longboat put off. His shots must have been heard, for the men in her were rowing like demons.

The Indians saw the boat coming, too. Half a dozen of them burst from the woods and raced for the rum barrel, thirst overcoming their fear. Bob might have shot at least one of them, but he held his fire. The range was too great for accuracy, and there was still a chance he would need all the bullets he had left. The Haidas made no attempt to carry the barrel away. They simply lay under the open bung and let the liquor pour into their mouths. When the boat's bow plowed up on the shingle, two of them ran away. The others were too drunk to stand.

Third Mate Snow was grim-faced when he saw what had happened to Langdon. He looked toward the woods as if he wanted to take revenge, but the barrage of arrows changed his mind.

"Hurry, now!" he said. "Get Mr. Langdon into the boat. Those furs'll make a soft bed for him. Then get aboard an' be ready to shove off. We'll cover you. Got to get out o' here before somebody else is hurt."

They carried the wounded man safely to the waiting boat while Snow and Bob sent a couple of shots toward the woods. Then the pair scrambled over the gunwale and they got away without further mishap. In a moment the oarsmen were pulling furiously for the ship.

*　　*　　*

Before that nightmare day ended, Bob Wingate wished he had never heard of sea otter skins. Nobody placed the blame on him, but his own conscience gave him torment far worse than the soreness of his shoulder wound, for Evan Langdon was dead. He regained consciousness just as they laid him on the deck of the *Javelin*, and his suffering was terrible to see. His teeth were clenched and great drops of sweat stood on his gray face.

There was no surgeon there to help, but Captain Sprague gave him morphine. It was obvious that the arrow must be pulled out. With a quick tug of his powerful hand, the captain jerked it from the wound. Langdon coughed once, the bright red arterial blood spraying from his lips. Then, with a brave effort at a smile, he was gone.

Bitterly Bob thought that afternoon of the man's kindness and patience—of the pains he had taken to teach the boys sound seamanship and navigation. Matt understood something of his friend's feeling and tried to comfort him.

"You did the best you could," he said. "Saved the rest o' the men, didn't you? It was that dirty sneak, Scully, that started the whole thing. If he hadn't been there, I bet there wouldn't have been any fighting. Gosh, how I wish I'd been there with you!"

Bob shook his head sadly. "There wasn't much anybody could do after it started," he said. "I should have known Scully was up to something, the way he hung around that chief. He must have been planning it from the minute he heard where we were headed—an' that was my fault."

It wasn't until the next day, when the clipper was a hundred miles out in the Pacific, that they held burial services for the first officer. In addition to the phrases in the prayer book, Sprague spoke briefly and from the heart. He had known Evan Langdon for many years and on many voyages. When he had finished, even the hard-shelled foremast hands were furtively wiping their eyes. Then, quietly, the canvas-wrapped body was slipped over the side into the Pacific.

As the ranks of sailors broke up, Snow came and summoned Bob to the quarterdeck. The captain was waiting for him there.

"Wingate," he said abruptly, "I've seen you're taking this pretty hard. No cause to feel that way. Langdon died in the line of duty, carrying out my orders. The way you handled it after he was hit does you credit. And you brought back the furs, which is what you were sent for. There'll be a tidy profit in that, for the owners and for those who shared in the venture. I think I'll give some of mine to Langdon's widow. If you feel it'll help any, you might want to do the same."

"Yes, sir," said Bob eagerly. "I'd been thinking of that myself."

"Good. Now there's one thing more. We're short a mate. Ordinarily we'd carry on as we are for the rest o' the voyage. But you showed the other day that you can think and act fast, and the men respect you. I'm going to promote you to fourth mate. Wyatt will take Langdon's place and the others'll move up. I'll be making it official pretty soon."

XIV

Bob was completely flabbergasted by the captain's words. The idea of a promotion so early in his career at sea had never entered his head.

He fumbled for words. "I'll try the best I know, sir," he said. Then Sprague shook his hand, and he walked away, hardly knowing where he went.

The announcement was made at noon. Shortly after Bill Wyatt finished taking his shot of the sun the crew was called aft. In his big, booming voice, the captain told them of the various changes in officer personnel, adding that he expected the same smartness and obedience they had shown earlier in the voyage. Some curious looks came Bob's way, but he squared his shoulders and set his jaw.

He had worried a little about how Matt would take the news. If the other boy felt any envy—and it was natural that he should—he concealed it well. With a delighted grin he came over to Bob and shook his hand.

"You sure rated it, Bob," he said. "Anything I can do to help, just say the word."

With Red Gilman, the bosun, it was somewhat different. Bob could tell from the scowl on his face that he felt he should have been chosen. The man said nothing to him directly, but Bob saw him whispering once or twice with some of the old hands in the crew. For the first day, at least, he avoided giving Gilman any orders. Meanwhile Preble, Snow, and Wyatt were especially cordial. They congratulated the new fourth mate and promised to back him up.

Three days' sail from Vancouver Island—it was New Year's Day, 1855—the first trouble appeared. They were in the edge of the northeast trades and beginning to pick up a strong wind from the port quarter. On orders from the afterdeck, Bob sent the men of his watch aloft to take in skysails. Most of them obeyed at once, but three men still loitered by the rail. One of them was a fellow named Davis, a squat, black-browed seaman who had been friendly with the dead Scully.

Bob advanced on the three, pulling a belaying pin out of the rack as he went.

"I said get aloft," he told them, trying to make his voice firm and steady.

Two of the men shuffled off uncertainly, but Davis merely grinned and spat over the rail. Bob felt a cold anger mounting in him.

"Davis," he said, "you've been asking for trouble. Now go aloft or you're going to get it."

The grin changed to a snarl, and Davis made a sudden lunge at him. If Bob hadn't been expecting it, he would have been knocked to the deck. As it was, he sidestepped in time and brought the heavy belaying pin down on the sailor's head. Davis went sprawling into the scuppers.

Bob whirled to face the others, but they were already hurrying up the ratlines. He went back and turned Davis over. The man opened dazed eyes and put up an unsteady hand to feel the huge lump starting to form on the side of his head.

Bob saw the bosun standing a few yards away. "Gilman," he said, "take this man to his bunk and make sure he's going to be all right." Then he turned on his heel, replaced the pin in the rack, and watched the work going on aloft.

If Gilman hadn't obeyed the command, he wasn't quite sure what he would have done. But the bosun followed orders. Five minutes later he came up to Bob and reported that Davis was doing as well as could be expected.

"I got to hand it to you, Mr. Wingate," he said grudgingly. "You settled that one real fast. Couldn't have done better myself. I reckon there won't be no more trouble."

Bob flushed as he heard the "Mister" for the first time. "Thanks, Red," he said. "I'll count on you."

Gilman was right. By prompt, firm action, the young mate had won not only the respect but the liking of the crew. Even Davis showed no more signs of insubordination. From that time on his authority went unchallenged.

*　　*　　*

They made a fast voyage to the Sandwich Islands, logging over three hundred miles on five successive days. The weather held clear for the most part, and the trade winds never failed them. On the seventeenth day from Vancouver Island—the twenty-third out of San Francisco—they sighted Diamond Head and swept into Honolulu Harbor under full sail.

It was the first time Bob had ever seen palm trees, and he stood by the rail, staring long at the waving fronds above the white ribbon of the beach. Outrigger canoes carrying brown-skinned men and maidens came flying out to meet the ship. Rich island voices laughed up at them, and some of the girls threw them flowers.

When they had dropped anchor among several whalers and merchantmen, the captain took Wing Lee ashore with him to buy fresh meat, fish, fruit, and vegetables and to arrange for taking on water. The little Chinese was a fixture aboard the *Javelin* now. Since being promoted to officer status, Bob was eating in the cabin, and he was amazed at the good food the steward served them. Sprague said more than once that he wished he could keep Wing Lee, though he had promised to let him leave the ship at the end of the voyage.

The Oriental's devotion to Bob was almost embarrassing. He frequently plied the young mate with extra helpings or with special dainties prepared for him alone. The second-hand uniform that Bob had drawn from the slop chest was kept in immaculate condition, washed and pressed and neatly mended. The boy felt he had been repaid many times over for fishing the poor fellow out of the bay.

Honolulu was a port every sailor liked to make. To the average foremast hand it meant carousing on native liquor in the water-front grogshops or seeking out the company of the good-natured, brown-faced women.

To Bob, looking at the island yearningly from the deck, it meant something else—a chance to explore exotic gardens or climb the jagged, dark mountains that hung like a backdrop behind the vivid colors of the town.

"Think any of us'll get ashore?" he asked Bill Wyatt. The newly appointed first mate grinned at him. "I shouldn't wonder," he replied. "We'll only be here two or three days, but I reckon you might rate a few hours' leave. I'd advise you to sheer off from the *wahines* an' the booze, though. Maybe there are better ways to prove you're a man."

Bob thanked him for the advice. "Those things aren't what I wanted, anyhow," he said, laughing. "I'd just like to see what a real tropical island's like."

He made it on the second day. Wearing his faded, brass-buttoned blue jacket and officer's cap, he went ashore in a boatload of twenty or thirty happy tars. Once off the dock he parted company with them. While they hurried to the nearest bar, he walked away from the water front till he reached a wide, tree-bordered road, flanked by government buildings and a few big frame residences.

Though it was mid-January, the air had a summery warmth, and the constant, gentle breeze carried the fragrance of a million flowers. They were all around him—huge red hibiscus blooms, pink and yellow and white flowers such as he had never seen.

He paused to look at the many-trunked banyan tree in the palace yard, and at that moment he heard a quick pounding of hoofs. Coming down the unpaved avenue at breakneck speed were four horses, ridden by whooping, laughing girls. Bob jumped for his life. He was barely out of the way when they thundered by. The girls were strapping, brown-skinned creatures with bright red flowers in their long black hair. They rode astride, without saddles, their Mother Hubbard dresses pulled up to give their strong bare legs free play.

He was still staring after them in astonishment when he heard a chuckle at his elbow. He looked around quickly into a pair of twinkling blue Yankee eyes. The young man who stood there was only a little older than himself and well dressed in the American fashion.

"Good morning," said the stranger. "I take it you're off one of the ships out there. Whaler, perhaps?"

"No," said Bob. "I'm in the *Javelin*—clipper out o' Boston."

The young man whistled. "I heard about her fast voyage," he said. "It's an honor to meet you. My name's Rodney Glenn, and I come from New Hampshire. I'd guess from your talk you must be a New Englander yourself."

It was Bob's turn to smile. "That's right—Kittery, Maine."

Glenn's eyes opened wide. "Kittery!" he cried. "Why that's only about ten miles from where I grew up—in Durham, on Great Bay! Portsmouth was our nearest big town, just as it must be yours. Do you have any plans for the rest

137

o' the day? If not, come on with me. I'd like to show you Honolulu. I'm at the MacNair shipyard. Mr. MacNair's my father-in-law."

As they walked toward the water front and the shipyard, Rodney Glenn talked. He told Bob how he had run off to sea in a whaler out of New Bedford, how a monster sperm whale had smashed his boat north of the island of Kauai, and how he had survived by swimming to shore on the rocky windward coast.

"It was touch an' go there, for a while," he said. "I'd have starved if it hadn't been for another castaway—a young Kanaka named Kokua. But we managed to get away after a few months, and I made it to Honolulu. You see there was a girl here—want you to meet her. She's Mahina Kea, Mac-Nair's daughter and my wife."

The shipyard disappointed Bob a little. All he saw on the ways were small schooners and a few whaleboats. But the place was busy. Husky Kanaka workmen sang as they swung axes or drove spikes.

"I've been around yards in Portsmouth," Bob said. "The *Javelin* was built there."

Glenn nodded. "No demand for big vessels here," he explained. "But we make a good living out of building smaller craft for island trading, and the whaleships are always in need of fresh boats."

He discussed the day's work with the yard foreman, gave a few orders, and led Bob to the little office, where he introduced him to Robert MacNair. The Scotsman was a vigorous man with hair beginning to gray, a pleasant smile, and an easy manner. It was evident that he had made a good life for himself here in the islands. He welcomed the young mate and suggested that Glenn take the afternoon off to entertain him.

Few Yankee sailors ever had the luck to be shown the

island of Oahu as Bob saw it. Glenn produced horses, and they rode eastward along the beach of Waikiki and out as far as the jutting promontory of Diamond Head. As they rode, he explained the politics of the Hawaiian people.

"The royal family's sort of run to seed since old Kamehameha the First conquered Oahu," he said. "The king lives in style, all right—spends most of the time holding parades and *luaus,* hunting, riding, and swimming. But the real prosperity of the islands is in the hands of a few white families—American and British. The Kanakas themselves are a lazy, happy people. They're content to let us make the plans and do the work. By good luck the whites who run things here are fine folks—churchgoers with a real sense of responsibility toward the natives. So we all get along well."

On their way back from the ride they stopped for a swim. Bob tried riding the huge rollers on a surfboard and was tossed heels over head. After that he marveled at the easy grace of the native boys, who came in erect, their lithe brown bodies in perfect balance.

It was five o'clock when they left Waikiki and rode to Rod Glenn's home. The pleasant, low-roofed house was set among great trees on the slope of Punch Bowl Hill. At its southern side, overlooking the harbor, was a broad, shaded porch—a *lanai,* as the Hawaiians called it. While Bob sat there, his host went inside. He reappeared a moment later, leading by the hand one of the most beautiful girls the young sailor had ever seen.

Mahina Kea Glenn was tall and slender, with a cloud of dark hair falling to her shoulders. Her skin was a warm, golden tan. And when she smiled, her generous, red-lipped mouth showed lovely teeth. The fact that she was barefoot seemed perfectly ladylike and natural, as did the blossoms in her hair and the length of flowered cotton she wore wrapped about her for a dress. Close behind her toddled a handsome little boy of two.

Glenn introduced them. The small son was named Robbie, after his grandfather.

They drank tall glasses of papaya juice while they talked. Bob told his host all the news he could think of about their part of New England while Glenn listened avidly.

"You'd think I was homesick, the interest I take," he said, laughing. "Maybe we'll go back there some day, but not for a long stay. This is where I want to live."

For dinner they ate fruit, followed by fish cooked in big green leaves, roast young pig, and a grayish-white, slightly sour paste called *poi*. It had to be eaten with the fingers, Mrs. Glenn explained, showing him how. The dessert was a beautiful golden-brown pie.

"I taught her how to make these," said her husband with a grin. "Every so often I get a hankering for New England vittles. We don't have apples here, but I think you'll find pineapple isn't such a bad substitute."

When the meal was over and the sun had set behind the mountains, Mahina Kea sang some native songs and danced a *hula*, her graceful hands moving softly to accompany the words.

Bob knew it would soon be ten o'clock, the time set for his return to the ship. He rose reluctantly to thank them and say good-by. "I hope there'll be other voyages," he said. "And I'd like to think I can always come to see you."

"Wait," Mahina Kea told him. "You must have a *lei*. When you sail out of the harbor, toss it overboard. That makes it sure that you'll come back."

She ran into the house and returned with a wreath of fragrant white ginger blossoms, which she hung about his neck.

"And this always goes with it," she said as, laughing, she

kissed him. "Don't forget to drop the flowers over the side, and Rod and Robbie and I will look for you on your next voyage."

Filled with the romantic beauty of the tropic night, Bob went down the hill and through the town to the waterside. Some of the sailors grinned at the sight of the *lei* around his neck, but he wore it proudly.

XV

Matt Ryder had been ashore on leave a day earlier, and they compared notes that night when they were on watch. With George Preble, Matt had ridden up to the top of the Pali—the mountain pass in the middle of the island.

"The other side of it," he told Bob, "there's a cliff that drops straight down, hundreds o' feet. They say the Oahu warriors that tried to stop King Kamehameha were chased clean over the cliff. Boy! The way the wind howls through there, I'd say some of 'em got *blown* over! The *Pali* makes a sort o' funnel, an' there's always a full gale across the top. You should have been with us."

Bob nodded. "Sounds mighty interesting," he said, "but I did all right. Ran into a fellow named Rod Glenn—practically a neighbor o' mine back home. We rode out to Diamond Head an' had a swim on the beach an' then a real Hawaiian dinner at his house. He used to be in a whaler an' got shipwrecked out here. Believe me, after hearing some o' his tales, I'll never look down on a whaleman again!"

The next morning the *Javelin* completed her provisioning and made ready to sail. With the anchor weighed, she was under full canvas by noon, making her stately way out of the harbor. Bob took a last sniff at the fragrant wreath of flowers and dropped it unobtrusively over the rail. Then the clipper headed westward along the sheltered southern coast.

Hong Kong lay nearly six thousand miles due west. The clipper *Game-Cock* had once made the run in nineteen days, averaging close to three hundred nautical miles a day all the way. But she must have had exceptional winds. No other ship had ever come close to that record in crossing the Pacific.

"I'll be satisfied with anything under thirty days for the voyage," Captain Sprague told his mates at mess, the second day out. "O' course, the quicker the better. If we can load tea before the first o' March, we can still count on the northeast monsoon. After that it's doubtful. Head winds would slow us up a lot on the run down to Java Head."

The trades favored them for three or four days. Then, somewhere near the 180th parallel, the winds grew fluky. They ran into warm, heavy rain that lasted a few hours, then a flat calm, broken that night by squalls from the southward. The yards had to be trimmed constantly and sail was being taken in or set around the clock. Bob was lucky if he got four hours sleep out of each twenty-four.

Sprague had the course altered to the northwestward, figuring they had gotten into the edge of the doldrums. After another day they picked up the trades again. With all sail set and drawing, they bowled along steadily till they sighted a small island off the southern tip of Formosa. That was on the twentieth day out of Honolulu, and it put them only five or six hundred miles from their goal.

"Day after tomorrow," Rodney Snow remarked that evening, "we ought to be picking up our China pilot. Ever seen a Chinese junk?"

Bob replied that he had seen pictures of them and they looked pretty clumsy.

"Don't fool yourself," Snow told him. "Awkward-looking, yes, but they're seaworthy, an' those coolies can sure handle the big bamboo sail. You'll be seeing plenty of 'em tomorrow."

Sure enough, the sun was hardly up when several of the queer craft appeared in the distance. Bob pointed them out to Wing Lee when he came out to dispose of a pan of scraps.

"Some o' your countrymen," Bob said. "I reckon they're fishermen. This China Sea's probably full of 'em."

"P'laps-so, fishermen," said the steward gravely. "Mebbe-so bad mans, come steal. Whatcha call 'em pilots."

Bob was amused. "No need to be afraid o' pilots, Wing Lee," he said. "They don't do any stealing. An' we'll need one to take us into port."

The little Chinese went off, mumbling to himself.

They sighted many more junks and a full-rigged ship or two during the rest of the day. As they neared the China coast, traffic grew thicker, and double lookouts were posted that night to avoid running down any small craft. Sprague had shortened sail as well, so that the clipper was logging less than ten knots. At dawn they sighted blue mountains to starboard, far off on the horizon.

Bill Wyatt had the quarterdeck when the forward lookout reported a sail approaching from the north.

"Stand by to heave to," the mate ordered. "This could be our Hong Kong pilot. If she's cutter-rigged, we can be sure." He took the spyglass from its rack beside the binnacle and trained it on the dot of sail.

"It's a big junk," Bob heard him say. "Looks like she wants to hail us though. Helmsman, put us up into the wind. Send the hands to the sheets, Wingate."

The *Javelin* wore around in answer to her helm and the sails were backed. The junk was tearing along rapidly now and less than a mile away. Suddenly Wing Lee burst out of the cabin and pattered toward Wyatt.

"Him pilot-ship!" he cried. "Come 'board an' cut thloat!"

The first mate laughed at him. "That's what we want, Wing," he replied. "If that's our pilot, we're in luck."

The wind was light and the sea not too rough. As the junk drew close, Bob watched her crew swing the huge square sail to bring her about, only fifty yards from the clipper's side. Now, he thought, they would lower a boat and send the pilot aboard. Instead, to his astonishment, the mats that covered the junk's hold were suddenly thrown back and a swarm of yelling men appeared. She was drifting nearer at an alarming rate. The half-naked Chinese along her rail brandished short, square-ended swords.

It came to Bob in a sickening flash that Wing Lee had known what he was talking about. "Pilots," of course, was his way of saying "pirates." He never had been able to pronounce an English "r."

Wyatt had already seen what was coming and barked an order. "Trim sail! Snap to it or we're in trouble!"

Red Gilman meanwhile had piped out all hands, and a score of men rushed to the braces. The junk was almost within jumping distance when the *Javelin* swung off to starboard and began to move. One of the pirates threw a grappling hook at that moment. It caught on the rail, and the crew of the Chinese craft howled in triumph.

Bob was nearest to it. He made one futile attempt to release the iron prong, but the yellow men were already hauling on it. His sheath knife was hanging at his belt. He whipped it out, leaned far over the rail, and slashed at the rope with all his might. Even as it parted, an ancient brass four-pounder aboard the pirate junk roared. The cannonball whistled past Bob's head, tore a hole in the foot of the main course, and plopped into the sea beyond. Before the old gun could be reloaded, the clipper was rapidly widening the gap. And a steady fire from the officers' Colts helped to discourage the screaming raiders.

Bob was still shaky as he clung to a shroud. He wiped the sweat out of his eyes with his sleeve and stared at the junk, now a good cable's length astern.

"Hey!" said Matt, at his elbow. "You're white as a sheet. They didn't hit you, did they?"

Bob shook his head and tried to laugh. "No," he answered. "But that shot was so close, I could feel the breeze. 'Pilots!' After this we'd better pay more attention to Wing Lee."

Captain Sprague had come on deck at the first shout of alarm and had witnessed the brief encounter. He ordered the ship back on course and stayed on the poop the rest of the morning, spyglass in hand. They sighted other junks but kept well clear of them.

At noon a trim little British cutter came out to meet them, and the real pilot was taken aboard. He was a grizzled old mariner with a Devonshire accent.

"Aye," he said gravely, when he heard about the pirate attack, "they've been givin' us a bit o' trouble. Ye've a fine, tall ship here, an' 'twould ha' been a pity to lose her."

Sprague snorted. "We'd have given 'em more'n they wanted in a fair fight," he answered. "What's wrong with Her Majesty's Navy? Why don't they clean these vermin out?"

"There's thousands o' junks along the coast here," said the pilot. "Board any one of 'em and all ye'll find is a peaceable fishin' craft. But the frigates do catch a few. Next time ye make port here, I'd advise ye to wait for a cutter flyin' the Union Jack."

That afternoon they anchored in Hong Kong Harbor, and the skipper went ashore. After the morning's incident a rack of cutlasses had been brought out and a strong guard was kept. Bob watched the swarms of sampans sculling about, hawking their wares of fish, fruit, and vegetables. He wondered how many of the harmless-looking coolies aboard them were potential pirates. Wing Lee, however, seemed to be easy in his mind about them.

He hailed the boats, pricing the produce in high-pitched Cantonese. After some haggling he asked Wyatt's permission to call one sampan alongside and made a few purchases.

"Velly fine cabbage," he explained to the mate. "And him plenty cheap."

When the captain returned, he called the mates together. "There's very little tea here," he said. "It's all up-river, at Canton. Half a dozen other ships are loading there, and we'll go up in the morning. I think we'll find a better market for our furs, too."

A Chunkiang River pilot came aboard early next morning and guided the clipper up the broad estuary. It took nearly all day to make the seventy miles to Canton, for the channel twisted back and forth like a snake, and junks and sampans crowded the water.

At sunset they found a mooring off the busy water front of the great South China port. Wing Lee had been standing by the rail, drinking in the sights and sounds and smells of his native city. Captain Sprague clapped him on the back.

"Hate to see you leave us," he told the little Chinese, "but a promise is a promise. Here's your pay. You can get your gear and come ashore with me."

Wing Lee's face was expressionless. He looked at the money and put it carefully in the pocket of his faded blue trousers. When the boat was lowered, he appeared with his belongings wrapped in a small bundle. Then he went to Bob and offered a slim yellow hand.

"You save life," he said. "Wing Lee not forgetting." And with that he descended the dangling rope ladder.

It was late that evening before Sprague came back to the ship. At breakfast—served this time by Absalom— he told the mates with some satisfaction that he had arranged for a profitable cargo of tea.

"We'll get top rates," he said. "Six pounds sterling per ton. And I figure to carry around eighteen hundred tons. There'll be two or three merchants coming aboard this morning to bid on our furs. I'll give you the job o' spreading 'em out so they'll show to advantage, Mr. Wingate."

Bob got Matt to help him, and they laid out the skins in neat piles. The sun gleamed on the sea otter pelts, and the river breeze ruffled the soft fur. Spread out on the quarterdeck they made a handsome show.

At ten o'clock several barges, rowed by smart-looking coolies in bright uniforms, pulled out from the docks. One by one they came alongside the ship and their owners were welcomed aboard. They were evidently very rich men, for their robes were all of the finest silk, handsomely embroidered, and their fingernails were like bird claws, inches in length.

There was a deal of bowing and scraping, and extravagant compliments were passed between the merchants and the courtly captain. They proceeded after that to examine the furs, their hands folded inside their wide sleeves, their plump faces completely impassive.

Sprague had dealt with Orientals before and knew there

was nothing to be gained by hurrying them. He stood patiently by the wheel, whistling a tune under his breath. Once, when the visitors' backs were turned, he gave Bob a solemn wink.

At last, when they had made a thorough appraisal, the captain invited them into his cabin and opened a bottle of old sherry. Bob wasn't present, but he could hear the polite conversation going on for a long time. Then they came out, bowing again, and their coolies were called to make up the skins into bundles, so many for each merchant.

When they had departed in their barges, Captain Sprague was in a mellow mood. He made no mention at the time of just how much had been paid for the fur, but Bob could see he was pleased. As he passed him, he gave the boy a pat on the shoulder.

"I reckon the owners'll say our cruise north was justified," he remarked. "Though after what happened up there, I won't be likely to try it again, even on orders."

The next day sampans began to come alongside, bringing big wicker chests of tea. The hatches were thrown open and tackle rigged for hoisting them over the side. All day long the winch pawls clicked as the crew swung the precious cargo aboard. Even through its tight wrappings, the tea had a fine, fragrant aroma.

It was midafternoon when Bob glanced down at one of the sampans and saw a familiar face among the boatmen. It was Wing Lee. He stood up and beckoned to the young mate.

"You gettum leave," he called. "Come 'long shoreside. Plenty good dinner my house."

Sprague granted him permission without hesitating. "The lad thinks a lot o' you, Wingate. You'd hurt his feelings if you didn't go. Just be sure you get back aboard tonight. I'll send a boat for you at ten o'clock."

As soon as the tea was hoisted aboard, Bob went down the ladder and got into the sampan to join his friend. Two men with long sweeps sculled the craft rapidly back to the docks, and soon the little Chinese and the tall young Yankee were walking side by side through the narrow, crowded streets. Little shops lined the pavements, and peddlers hawked their wares in high, singsong voices. Every minute or two the pair had to jump out of the way of coolies pulling little two-wheeled carts, piled high with food, firewood, or other merchandise, and racing along at breakneck speed. Strange smells and sounds came out of the packed tenements behind the bazaars.

Wing Lee steered Bob through a maze of alleys till they were half a mile from the water front. There he led him into a hallway, cool, quiet, and half dark. "This house of my father," he said proudly. "Name Wing Chee Fong."

They entered a room that made Bob stare in surprise. It was fairly large and beautifully furnished. A rich-colored, silky rug covered the floor, and there were carved chests and chairs and lacquered screens. After a moment Wing Chee Fong came in. He was a thin, scholarly-looking gentleman in a long embroidered coat. On his head was a black skull cap, and he wore steel-rimmed spectacles that gave his face an owlish look. He bowed low and welcomed his son's friend while Wing Lee translated his words and Bob's reply.

A demure Chinese girl shuffled in bearing a tray with rice wine in tiny cups. When she was gone, they sat there sipping the mild drink and trying to carry on a conversation. The preliminaries concerned Bob's health and that of his family. Then the older man went on to thank him in flowery language for saving his unworthy son and to wish him wealth and good fortune. Bob did his best to return the compliments, belittling his own part in the rescue and praising Wing Lee's talents as a steward. He was relieved when the difficult conversation ended and dinner was served.

A full-course Cantonese dinner, he discovered, was practically a day's work in itself. The dishes brought in seemed endless in number and variety. Most of them he found delicious, though he had little idea of what they contained. The meats surely included chicken and pork, and he recognized eggs and shrimp. There were mushrooms, too, and bean sprouts, and of course rice. Tea was served with every course, in dainty cups without handles.

Oddly enough, for all the immense quantity, Bob finished the repast feeling well filled but not uncomfortable as he had sometimes been at home after a Thanksgiving dinner.

He tried to express his thanks to Wing Lee's father, and then, after a polite interval, the young Chinese escorted him back to the dock. It wasn't yet ten o'clock, and they stood there awhile, waiting for the *Javelin*'s boat.

"What time you sail off?" Wing Lee asked.

"A couple o' days, I guess—soon as we've got our cargo. Wish you were coming with us. I'd like to take you home for some New England food. I don't mean it's any better'n yours, but it's different."

Wing Lee grinned. "Mebbe-so sometime I come 'long 'Melica-side," he said. "But no stop Flisco!"

XVI

Captain Sprague supervised the careful stowing of the tea chests as they were swayed down the hatches. He hadn't been able to find another steward, but he was pleased at the progress that had been made. It was still only the twelfth of February, and the winter monsoon blew strong from the northeast.

"Ought to make a fast passage," he told the mates, rubbing his big hands and looking at the weather. "If we make it in ninety days or less, there's an extra bonus offered in London—one pound premium per ton! That's nearly ten thousand dollars. Worth going after, eh?"

Another race appeared to be shaping up, as well. Two other American clippers, the *Fortune* and the *Western Star,* were loading tea at the same time. And a 1,250-ton Britisher, the *Cairngorm,* built in 1853 to rival the Yankees with her sharp clipper lines, was also in the anchorage.

Actually it was the *Cairngorm* that completed her cargo first. She dropped down the river with flags flying on the thirteenth, while several sampan-loads of tea still had to come aboard the *Javelin.* Sprague was unconcerned. "We'll catch her in the Indian Ocean," he prophesied. "Never saw a British skipper yet that dared to carry full sail in any kind o' wind."

The last chest came aboard by lantern light that night, and preparations were made to leave on the morning tide. Bob took advantage of the final night in port to get a solid eight hours' sleep. He knew he would be lucky to catch half that once they put to sea. At dawn he was on deck once more, making sure all hatches were battened down, sails up in gaskets, and everything shipshape. With full tide at nine o'clock they had to be ready to take advantage of the ebb.

A cable's length away, upstream, similar preparations were being made aboard the *Western Star*. The *Fortune* was still loading tea, her crew working like demons to hoist it aboard, but with little chance to get away on the same tide. At eight-thirty Captain Sprague was on the quarter-deck. He paced back and forth, sniffed the breeze, and watched the water that eddied past the hull. Just as he was ready to order the hands aloft, Bob looked toward shore. There was a small sampan coming rapidly in the direction of the ship.

He watched till he was sure it was headed for them, then hailed the poop. "Somebody wants to board us, Captain," he called.

"Can't be helped," Sprague growled. "No time to waste. Tide'll turn any minute, an' we've got to weigh anchor."

The boat was only a few hundred feet away now, and Bob got a good look at its single passenger in the stern sheets. "It's Wing Lee, sir!" he cried.

The captain stared at the sampan, then grinned. "Hold it there at the capstan!" he ordered. "You, Wingate, drop the ladder."

"Aye, aye, sir!" said the young mate happily, and ran to the rail to welcome his Chinese friend.

"You take me back now for voyage 'Melica-side?" asked Wing Lee hopefully. He seemed to doubt the answer and stayed in the boat till he heard it from Sprague's own lips.

"Come on!" roared the skipper. "You're a nuisance, but we'll sign you on again."

He was still chuckling while the Chinese scurried up the side. Then he greeted him with a stern face. "No more

jumping ship," he warned, and shook Wing Lee's hand. Then he swung around to face the deck.

"Come on, you lubbers!" he roared. "Spring to it, now! Give us a chantey there, up for'ard!"

To the chorus of "Blow the Man Down," the capstan began to turn, while loosened gaskets let out the folds of canvas. Within minutes the anchor was catted and the sails sheeted home. The tide was just at the turn.

Looking across the water, they could see canvas blossoming out on the *Western Star*. This would be a real race, with an even start. The *Javelin's* river pilot had caught some of the crew's excitement. He was a middle-aged Chinese, wise in the twisting vagaries of the channel. Ordinarily his face would have been solemn, but now his eyes twinkled and his teeth showed in a grin. He took the clipper westward across the bows of the *Western Star,* and by the maneuver they got out of the lee of the land. The fitful breeze was from the northeast. It caught the flat-trimmed sails and sent them into a ten-length lead before their rival could make the same move.

Throughout the afternoon the other ship hung on in their wake, with practically no change in their positions. Both clippers arrived off Hong Kong before sunset and dropped their pilots at the same time. Then they squared away with the wind astern for the run down the South China Sea. When Bob's watch turned in at midnight, he could still see the other clipper's running lights off the starboard quarter.

The monsoon picked up force during the night. At dawn they were driving southward at fifteen knots, every stitch of canvas straining to the utmost. It was a glorious sight to see the towering white sails of the *Western Star* a scant mile astern. That was how they ran throughout the morning. Then a sudden squall obscured the sea around them and tons of rain fell on the deck.

When it cleared after an hour, the other clipper had dropped farther behind. She was hull down, but from the look of her upper spars, her skysails had either been blown out or taken in. By luck and daring the *Javelin* had come through undamaged.

They logged a splendid three hundred and thirty miles between that noon and the next. Bob had wondered about the ship's speed, loaded as she was. Her freeboard was several feet less than it had been when they left San Francisco. Troubled, he had asked George Preble about it.

"Don't worry, boy," the third mate told him. "She's built for it. A cargo like this may cut a knot off her top speed, but she'll handle better than she did in ballast, an' ride easier, too."

When he took a turn at the wheel during his watch, Bob found that it was true. The clipper had less tendency to yaw, and she didn't heel as far to the quartering wind. The course was due south, keeping to windward of the Paracels. After those islands lay safely astern, Captain Sprague ordered a shift of a point or two to the westward.

That was on their third day out of Hong Kong. The monsoon held steady, giving the *Javelin* all the wind she could handle without shortening sail, and day after day she was logging better than three hundred miles. Early on the fifth day they sighted Great Natoena to port and drove on south toward the equator and the Java Sea.

Now the skipper spent most of his time on deck. He had known these waters from boyhood, when he sailed out of Salem on an East Indiaman. At table in the cabin he often mentioned the great record made by the *Witch of the Wave* in 1852. Like the *Javelin* she was Portsmouth-built, and with a January monsoon to push her along, she had sailed from Canton to Java Head in the extraordinary time of seven days, twelve hours.

"Our wind may not be quite as strong," he told the

mates, "but so far we're right on the heels o' that record. Keep your fingers crossed. An' keep an eye peeled for that Britisher ahead."

The sixth day passed, and dawn of the seventh found them scudding south with the coast of Sumatra off to starboard, somewhere beyond the horizon.

Bill Wyatt was wearing a broad grin at breakfast. "If this wind holds," he told the others, "I won't have to take a sight today. We'll be in Sunda Strait by noon."

The crew had caught the thrill of it now, and all hands stayed on deck, though there was little work to be done at the ropes. Red Gilman kept them busy with holystones and paintpots. But even so, they spent a lot of their time watching the sea ahead. At eleven o'clock the foremast lookout spotted a distant dot of canvas, and everyone rushed to the rail.

Wyatt went aloft with the glass. "It's the *Cairngorm!*" he called down. "She's under royals but that's all. Wait— she's sighted us now! She's breaking out skysails. And that looks like land beyond her!"

Bob held his impatience in check. He would have given a lot to be up there at the topgallant crosstrees with a view over the heaving waves, but his duties kept him on deck. Finally the loom of a distant blue headland was visible off the port bow.

"There it is," Sprague called out. "That's the Head! We'll be abeam by noon—seven days an' three hours out o' Canton!"

Bob drew a deep breath. This was one of the moments he had dreamed about—his first view of Java Head. For down-East sailormen it had been a landmark for more than a hundred years. And to see it on a record-breaking voyage! Here he was—mate of a Boston clipper as fast as any ship that ever sailed. What more could a New England youngster ask?

Matt came up beside him at the lee rail. His eyes were aglow with the same excitement. "How's it feel to be only halfway 'round the world from home?" he asked.

"Fine," said Bob. "I see we're hauling up on the *Cairngorm,* too. Guess they were feeling pretty proud o' themselves—making Java Head in eight days. You an' I'll have something to brag about when we get into port."

They drove up to leeward of the British clipper till the two ships were running side by side, only a couple of cables' lengths apart. At Sprague's orders the *Javelin* dipped her colors, and the salute was returned. Then they were surging on by. They led her through the jaws of the Strait, and beyond was the broad expanse of the Indian Ocean.

Once they were through, the monsoon, broken by the land, lost some of its force. It blew lightly that afternoon, and the captain ordered studding sails set on the fore and main yards, giving the ship greater spread of sail. Then, in the first night watch, they ran into the area of uncertain winds. Puffs seemed to come from the east, southeast, or northeast by turns.

The crew, spoiled by lack of work during the past week, grumbled as they sweated the yards around. Sometimes a shift of course was called for every few minutes, and all hands were kept on deck most of the night. To Bob it seemed that all their earlier speed would go for nothing. But the older mates didn't share his concern.

"Wind'll probably steady from the southeast soon." Snow yawned as they went to their bunks at four in the morning. "Anyhow, with the start we got, a ninety-day passage doesn't look too hard."

They were routed out again at eight for a hasty breakfast and more work at the braces. Then in midmorning the fluky breeze died out completely. All day they rolled to the oily ocean swells, with slack ropes slatting and sails drooping from the yards. The sight taken at noon showed they had made only fifty miles in the twenty-four hours since passing Java Head.

By the time the sudden tropical darkness shut down, the heat was almost stifling. Nobody slept inside that night. Panting and dripping with perspiration, the men sprawled on the open deck, stripped almost naked. Bob was standing with the helmsman at the idle wheel when the captain strolled up. He cast an eye at the stars, above the mizzen top, and the glow from the binnacle lamp showed a grin on his rugged face.

"Let 'em sleep," he said. "They'll wake up quick enough when it starts to rain." And with that he sauntered off and went back to his cabin.

Bob was nonplussed. Rain? Overhead the stars were still blazing bright in the hot night. But when he looked eastward, he realized that there were no stars—only a heavy pall of blackness. Another hour went by. There was no wind to foretell the downpour, no lightning or thunder. It came wholly without warning—a few big drops, followed instantly by solid sheets of rain, falling vertically.

There were howls of dismay through the roar of water on the deck. In seconds everybody was wet to the skin. Bob remembered then. He had heard old tars speak with awe of Indian Ocean cloudbursts. This one lasted only an hour, but when it was over, he found what had been an empty bucket standing by the scuttle butt was full and running over. He estimated that more than ten inches had fallen during the shower.

The ship still lay becalmed, hardly rolling now that the sea had been flattened by the downpour. The sails dripped, and tons of water went gurgling off through the scuppers. At least Bob's clothes had had a good rinsing. When he went to his little cabin at the end of the watch, he wrung them out and hung them up to dry.

A little before dawn he half woke, sensing that something

had changed. Instead of the soft slap of water against the sides, there was a rushing sound as it curled past. A creak of taut cordage came from above. And the first gray light coming through the porthole showed his clothes hanging out at a slant from the bulkhead. The ship was heeled to starboard, her wet canvas drawing to a good breeze. All these things gave him a feeling of well-being. He grinned, rolled over, and went back to sleep.

XVII

With the southeast trades abeam, the *Javelin* plowed steadily west by south toward Africa. The Indian Ocean, Bob found, was a very big and lonely place. Only once, after leaving Java Head, did they sight another sail. That was on their twentieth day out, somewhere near Mauritius.

The lookout reported two ships, apparently hove to, a few miles ahead. As the clipper drew nearer, it was easy to see that the vessels were whalers, squat and short-masted, with canvas stained gray by years at sea. They had half a dozen boats out, and even from a distance the reason was obvious. All around them, for miles, the ocean was filled with whales. There must have been hundreds of the monsters, for everywhere Bob looked he could see the steamy white bushes of their spouting.

All hands aboard the *Javelin* lined the rail to watch as they swept past. Two boats were fast to whales and being towed rapidly through the water. Even as the clipper's seamen cheered, one of the great black shapes breached close to a boat, and the tiny figure in the bow drove home his lance. How the battle ended, Bob never knew, for the *Javelin* rapidly widened the distance and the whaleships were soon hull down astern.

The southeast trades carried them across the Tropic of Capricorn. Then they entered a belt of squally, changeable winds—the horse latitudes. The crew, after nearly two weeks in which they could loaf, whittle, read, or play cards in their spare time, now suddenly found themselves busy day and night. The oldtimers took it in stride. But Bob had to be firm with some of the newer men. It took three days to whip them back into shape, and he got little sleep during that time.

By dint of shifting the yards every hour or two and keeping all the sail on that the ship could carry, they managed to log better than two hundred miles a day. Captain Sprague said they were making fair progress, but with the ninety-day bonus in mind he pushed the mates, the crew, and the clipper hard.

In one way it was fortunate he did. By the time they neared the Cape of Good Hope they had a taut ship. Day after day now they tacked into the teeth of the westerlies—the same world-circling winds they had bucked off Cape Horn. And in latitude 40° South the weather worsened. The skipper came on deck one morning, looked at the sky, and barked out an order to shorten sail. There were ominous black clouds banking up on the western horizon.

The men rushed aloft and worked like Trojans. Within half an hour the yards were stripped to topsails, a single jib, and the spanker on the mizzen. They finished just in time. With a roar like a thousand lions the wind struck them. The fore-topsail split squarely down the middle and flared out in streaming tatters. Then, with a sudden shift, the gale came out of the south, laying the clipper over till her starboard scuppers were awash.

"It's a bull's-eye squall!" Wyatt yelled above the uproar of the wind. "We'll catch it from astern next!"

Bob never knew what the velocity of that storm was, but the wind force was greater than anything in his brief experience. Literally he had to cling to a stay with all his strength to keep from being blown overboard. When gusts came from the east, the ship staggered drunkenly down into the trough and was nearly pooped by the following sea.

Then she tilted her nose up till her bowsprit was pointing at the black and squally sky.

Violent as it was, the storm was over in less than an hour. The wind died, but mountainous waves continued to crash down on the ship, seemingly from all directions.

"Get aloft," the captain ordered. "Take that fore-topsail off her an' run up a new one. Set the courses an' to'gallants."

With the masts swinging back and forth in a perilous arc, the topmen clung to their perches and somehow made sail. Bob heaved a sigh of relief when all of them returned safely to the deck. At once they were put to work hauling the yards around, for a fresh breeze had sprung up from the southwest.

With the wind now abeam, the *Javelin* labored through the big seas on a northwest course, clawing her way off the lee shore of Africa. The next day it was possible to add more sail, and soon she was carrying topgallant sails and royals. Her position, on March 23, was 13° East and 33° South. The bull's-eye squall off the Cape had cost valuable distance, and Sprague wanted no more delays.

On the twenty-fifth the breeze steadied from south by east, giving the clipper a chance to pile up knots on her course toward the islands of St. Helena and Ascension. But hardly had she settled to her gait when a lookout reported a sail astern.

The captain sent Wyatt aloft with the glass, and in the same breath he ordered skysails set. Within five minutes the identity of the oncoming ship was certain. Hard as it was to believe, she was the *Western Star*, roaring after them under full canvas.

Sprague grinned. "All right, Cap'n Douglas," he said, "you've been looking for a race an' now you've got it."

Now that her skysails were set, the *Javelin* appeared to hold her lead. When she had left the other ship astern in the China Sea, all the officers had forgotten about her. This new development had them speculating on how she had overhauled them.

"I just won't believe she's got as much speed as we have," said Snow. "Must be she sailed around that calm that hit us outside Sunda Strait. Or else she came along past the Cape o' Good Hope just late enough to miss the squall."

But whatever special luck the *Western Star* might have had, she continued to hold her position a bare three miles astern. For the rest of that day the pursuer remained in sight. Not till after dusk did Captain Sprague take any further action. Then, as soon as it was dark, he ordered studding sails set. The breeze held steady, and the added sail gave the ship an extra knot of speed.

"All right," he said grimly. "Let's see if she's still in sight when morning comes."

The crew had welcomed the excitement of the race, as they would any break in the monotony. Among the watch on deck a few small bets had been laid before dawn, though only one or two men were willing to wager on the *Western Star*. As soon as it grew light enough to see the horizon, all hands stared up anxiously at the lookout in the mizzen top.

"Hey, Mike—what's the word?" they yelled at him.

But with a sense of his own importance the man kept silent for long minutes. Finally it was the first mate who hailed him and he answered.

"Hard to make out, sir," he said, "but there's somethin' off the sta'board quarter. Looks like a sail. Aye, sir—now she's clear. It's her, right enough, an' she's got her stuns'ls on, just like us."

Wyatt swore under his breath and eyed the set of the canvas on the *Javelin*'s lofty spars. At breakfast the officers discussed the race.

"Sticking to us like a leech, sir," said Wyatt to the captain. "Changed her course a bit to leeward in the night an' I reckon she gained a mile or so. She's off the starboard quarter now."

Sprague nodded but didn't seem upset. "She's only got fifteen hundred tons of tea aboard," he told them. "Before the wind that would help her. Must be the reason she's bearing out farther to leeward. We'll sail our own course. I've seen ships trapped in the Gulf o' Guinea before now."

All morning the rival clipper stayed in the same relative position, though she seemed to be pulling still farther to the eastward. Late in the afternoon she dropped out of sight below the starboard horizon.

"Well," said Red Gilman, "I'm glad to see her go. Now maybe we can get some work out o' you lubbers!" And since there was little to be done aloft or at the braces, he set them to swabbing decks.

*　　　*　　　*

Daily the sun shone and the wind blew fair. The *Javelin* logged her three hundred miles as steadily as a clock. Bob, usually helped by Matt, had been given charge of the log line, and he made his hourly readings with conscientious care. One thing puzzled him. When the position was taken with the sextant each day, they seemed to have advanced farther than the dead reckoning would allow. He didn't like to bring it up with the other mates for fear they would say his knot count was at fault. At last he went to the chart-room and studied Maury's wind and current charts. Then the difficulty explained itself.

For a week now they had been in the Benguela Current —the strong, invisible push of water northward off the African coast. If it was moving at even two or three knots, the log line would read that much under their true forward speed.

While he was at it, the young mate satisfied himself about the currents they would be encountering farther north. He found that somewhere a few hundred miles below the great bulge of West Africa, the Benguela Current swung westward and merged with the South Equatorial Current, running toward Brazil. But deeper in the Gulf of Guinea both winds and currents came from the west. That must have been what the captain meant when he talked about ships being "trapped."

What would he do if he were captain of a clipper in their position? How would he maneuver to beat the fast-sailing *Western Star*? Judging by the charts, he thought they could expect to run out of wind soon after they crossed the equator. The chart showed a belt of a few hundred miles there, labeled "Doldrums." Then, somewhere below the Cape Verde Islands, they would be picking up the edge of the northeast trades. He wondered if it might be sound strategy to sail northwestward with the trades abeam, heading out into mid-Atlantic instead of battling contrary winds all the way up the West African coast to Spain and the Bay of Biscay. It would mean more actual distance to cover, but he thought it might save time.

A teen aged ship's boy acting as fourth mate was hardly in a position to make any suggestions to a veteran skipper, so he kept his mouth shut and waited for developments. When they had passed a hundred miles or so to the east of Ascension Island, the captain ordered the course changed two points to the west. This was right in line with Bob's amateur thinking, and he congratulated himself. Some of the foremast hands didn't like it as well. They would have been happier to stay within possible sighting distance of the other clipper, for most of their bets still stood.

The wind held strong all the way to the equator, and they went over it on the morning of April 15. That was

Bob's fourth crossing of the line, so he got no particular thrill from it. At noon the sight gave their position as longitude 17° West. It was two days later that the wind faltered and gave out.

There followed a trying time when the ship rocked lazily under a blazing sun, the sea heaving hot and oily around her. The crew sweated and growled. Some of them dropped lines overboard, but no fish rose to their bait. It was as if everything in that stagnant ocean had died.

Late on the second windless day, Bob saw Wing Lee come out of the steward's pantry with a chunk of spoiled meat and a long, coiled line. He was the only officer on deck at the time.

"You think you're going to catch something with that?" Bob laughed. "Nobody else has had any luck at all."

The little Chinese smiled and said nothing. He stuck the meat on a huge hook and fastened a lead weight below it. Then he started letting the line down over the taffrail. Fathom after fathom it ran out, till the bait was three hundred feet below. Meanwhile, Wing Lee had made the upper end fast to the rail. He stood there with his hand on the line, and suddenly there was a tug that made the knot creak. Hastily the steward tried to haul in, his thin arms straining at the heavy cord.

"You come quick help!" he panted, and Bob hurried to his aid.

The thing at the other end of the line was powerful and angry. It thrashed mightily and rushed to and fro. For several minutes they made little headway, and Bob feared the line would break. Then at last the creature on the other end seemed to tire a little. Bob called Red Gilman, and the three of them hauled the catch upward, hand over hand. When it was fifteen or twenty feet from the surface, the brute got a new lease on life. There was a tremendous tugging and shaking on the line. It was all they could do to hold on.

Bob managed a quick look into the turbulent water. "It's a shark!" he gasped. "Big one, too!"

More men had run up now, and several added their strength to the pull. Matt stood by with an ax. When they finally dragged the writhing eight-foot monster over the rail, he swung a powerful stroke at the back of its head, stunning it for a moment, and quick knives finished the job.

Red Gilman stared at the beast in disgust. "Why couldn't it be somethin' we could eat?" he growled and turned away.

But Wing Lee's yellow face was wreathed in smiles. He brought a huge butcher knife from the pantry. "Me cut off fins," he announced. "Make plenty good soup!"

Bob shuddered. "You think anybody'll eat it?" he asked. "Not me!"

Absalom came and looked and shook his head. His eyes were round and white in his black face. "What a lookin' thing!" he moaned. "Dem big teeth! Mus' be some kin' o' debbil, ah reckon!"

Wing Lee paid no attention to his critics but proceeded to cut away the big back fin and carve it into small pieces. By the time he finished he had more than a peck. Then he took over the cook's big galley pot, put in potatoes, onions, and some of his own Chinese seasoning, and proceeded to cook shark's fin soup. At Bob's order the crew heaved the mutilated body back over the side.

The soup—it was actually more like a stew—was served at supper in the cabin that night. Captain Sprague sniffed the savory aroma of the dish, turned some of the pieces over with his spoon, and looked puzzled.

"What you got here, China Boy?" he asked.

"This velly fine soup, Canton-style," Wing Lee replied

proudly. "Mist' Bob he eat some, my house. You taste, sir."

The captain and mates took cautious nibbles, then ate with relish. Out of loyalty to his friend Bob tried the concoction and found it delicious.

"Mmm," said Sprague. "Got another helping o' that, Wing Lee? Tastes sort o' like shrimp, only better. Some kind o' fish, I reckon, though I didn't know anybody'd had that much luck today."

Wing Lee acknowledged the compliment with a solemn little bow, and Bob nearly choked as he tried to keep his laughter to himself.

XVIII

A little breeze sprang up at dawn of the third day. It blew from the east, and even though it was a warm wind, it took away some of the oppressive, steamy heat they had had to endure.

"We'll see," said the skipper. "This may peter out. But if it holds steady, we're beginning to catch the nor'east trades. Trim the yards an' we'll steer a course due north."

The wind blew harder hour by hour, swinging more northerly, and the ship plunged ahead like a race horse under the whip. She was pointing as high as she could, but the drift of the current gave her two knots of westing for every ten she made northward. After a couple of days of brisk sailing they had reached a latitude of 15° North and were some two hundred miles west of the Cape Verdes.

What had become of the *Western Star?* There was a good deal of speculation among the mates and the crew. Perhaps she had avoided the doldrums by keeping close to Africa. If so, she might well have stolen a lead before now. Captain Sprague, however, appeared less worried than any of them. He stuck to the same northerly course as day followed day, and nodded with satisfaction when Bob reported the log each hour.

Two weeks after crossing the equator the *Javelin* had passed to the west of the Azores and was almost in the middle of the North Atlantic. The northeast trades had lost some of their driving force now. On the last day of April the ship entered a belt of uncertain, shifting winds. For twenty-four hours the yards were trimmed half a dozen times in every watch. Some of the crew, soft-handed after a long stretch of easy sailing, cursed at the blisters that formed on their palms.

Then, little by little, there came a steadying in the breeze. It blew out of the west, warm and humid off the Gulf Stream. Showers came with it. Spare sails were stretched to catch some of the rain, and Bob had a chance to wash the salt off his body in fresh water. Wing Lee washed the officers' clothes and hung them on a line, forward of the mizzenmast. Almost as soon as they were in place, the sun broke through and a booming westerly wind sent the clipper toward the coast of Europe at a glorious fifteen knots.

Studying the chart, Bob figured they were then some fifteen hundred miles from the mouth of the English Channel. At this rate, and barring accidents, they might hope to reach it in five or six days!

They were now seventy-five days out of Canton. Captain Sprague's face was still rock-hard when he was within sight of the crew, but in the privacy of the cabin he unbent enough to smile occasionally. Once he told Bob that he had a small wager on with the master of the *Western Star.*

"Will Douglas is a first-class skipper," he said. "He won't be making many mistakes, an' he's sailing a course that's a bit shorter than ours. Now that we've got the westerlies, though, I figure we're making more knots."

The fine booming wind held. After two days a ship was sighted off the port bow, moving eastward on a course that converged with their own. And as soon as they had her fairly abeam, it was possible to see her gleaming black hull and the house flag at her truck.

"She's a packet," Bill Wyatt announced. "Train's Liverpool Line. From the looks of her, I'd say she's McKay-built. Might be the *Daniel Webster.*"

The packet liner was carrying plenty of sail, but it soon became apparent that she was no match for the *Javelin.* When the two vessels were a mile apart, Bob took a look at her through the telescope. Brasswork glinted in the sun, and her well-painted deck structures were dazzling white. Passengers lined the rail to watch the great clipper pull ahead, yard by yard. At sunset the Liverpool packet was only a dot on the horizon astern.

On they sailed, and on the sixth of May the noon sight showed their position as 49° North and only 8° 30' West. The entrance to the English Channel lay right ahead, and a feeling of certain triumph swept through the ship.

"What a voyage!" Bob told Matt Ryder exultantly. "We'll pass the Lizard tonight, an' then all we have to do is run up the Channel to the Thames. Just another five hundred miles!"

His words were barely spoken when the wind shifted. It came in puffs from the north, and all hands were set to trimming the yards. Then a bank of gray cloud built up ahead. Before sunset they were beating up against a strong head wind, and most of the sky was darkly overcast.

That night the clipper pitched and rolled, buffeted by choppy Channel seas that met the long, eastward-running Atlantic swells. For the first time in months Bob felt a touch or two of seasickness. However, he ate his supper and stood his watch. Now that he was a mate, he would have died before letting anybody know how his stomach felt. The upper sails had been furled, and the ship was under topgallants now. She was making short tacks, coming about at least once in every hour. Bob was soon too busy to think about any uneasiness, and by the time he turned in at midnight he was much better.

All next day the storm continued. They bucked into rain squalls and gusts of wind, and the flying scud made it hard to see ahead. Once a French fishing boat came out of the swirling mist almost under their bows and went skittering off to the southward with a frightened crew cursing and shaking their fists.

Captain Sprague took the weather philosophically. "No ship can expect fair winds every day," he remarked at supper. "We've had our share o' luck. Now we've just got to make what headway we can."

By dead reckoning they had made only about a hundred miles of easting in the last two days. And the third day—May 9th—was just as bad. At this rate, Bob figured despondently, they would never reach London Docks in time to collect their bonus.

At noon on the tenth the rain and driving fog showed a break to the north. They were on the starboard tack at the time, running toward the English coast. Through the gap in the clouds the foremast lookout sighted land, and Wyatt, hurrying aloft with the glass, identified the headland as Portland Bill. Almost at the same moment the sails of a tall ship appeared off their port quarter. As soon as the first mate turned his telescope on her, he gave an excited shout.

"She's the *Western Star*!" he called. "Under royals an' coming up fast!"

From the quarterdeck Captain Sprague sent the other mates into sudden action. "Get the royals on her!" he bellowed. "Then stand by to come about."

It took only minutes to release the royal gaskets and get the sails drawing. Immediately afterward the yards were hauled around and the clipper squared away on the port tack. Meanwhile, the weather had shut down once more, and their rival was out of sight in the mist.

An anxious watch was kept that night, for with the added speed of the sail they were carrying, there was real danger of a collision. Just before dawn the wind began to shift. It was coming now from a little north of east and the rain was slackening. At eight o'clock the *Western Star* became visible once more. She was three or four miles off the port beam, and beyond her they could see the Isle of Wight looming up faintly.

In the intervals of trimming the yards, all eyes were on the other ship. "Hey!" called Snow suddenly. "Look at her now! She's heading in past the point—making for Portsmouth!"

Captain Sprague studied her actions through the glass. "Hmm," he muttered. "Her orders are for London Docks, same as ours. There's only one reason she'd put in at Portsmouth. Cap'n Douglas must figure this storm's going to last. There's probably only one tug for hire in the harbor there, an' if he can charter it to tow him up-Channel, he thinks he'll beat us in. All right—I'm gambling on the weather! Keep her as she is, you there at the wheel."

Sure enough, before noon they saw a cloud of smoke coming up astern, and through it they could make out the upper spars of the clipper. As long as the wind held easterly, the *Javelin* was still forced to tack, and the steamboat and her tow overhauled them steadily.

Once, on the port tack, they were within hailing distance of the *Western Star* and could hear the jeers of the men along her rail. Most of the other clipper's canvas had been clewed up to make the towing easier, so her crew had little to do but gloat.

Then, in midafternoon, when she had pulled a mile or so ahead, patches of blue sky appeared between the clouds and the breeze backed into the south. The skipper grinned and rubbed his big square hands together. "Up aloft there, you lubbers!" he roared. "Lay on skysails an' stuns'ls. We'll see who gets to London first!"

The south wind steadied and grew stronger—a fine quartering breeze that heeled the clipper over to port and sent her charging along at twelve knots or better. The smoke cloud was no longer ahead but abeam. Then it began drop-

ping rapidly astern as the seamen on the *Western Star* struggled frantically to set their sails and cast off the towing cable.

*   *   *

It was the morning of May 12 when the *Javelin* rounded the North Foreland. She was guided by the pilot who had come aboard at Dungeness, in the night, answering their blue signal lamp. The first light of the morning sun had struck the white cliffs with dazzling brightness as they passed Dover. Now they had reached the broad mouth of the Thames River. At eleven they were taken in tow by a steam tug, and by midafternoon the clipper was berthed. Captain Sprague went ashore at once to see that the time of their arrival was officially recorded. Eighty-seven days wasn't the fastest voyage ever made from Canton, but it was good enough to earn a premium on the cargo.

Even more important to the pride of the officers and men was the fact that they had beaten the *Western Star*. The other clipper hove in sight about dusk, and her men had very little to say.

Captain Douglas came over to pay his respects—and his wager—that evening. "Well, Jonathan," Bob heard him say, "you outguessed me that time. Reckon if I hadn't put into Portsmouth for a tow, we might have trimmed you. It would have been a tight race, anyhow."

"Just luck," Sprague chuckled, "that the wind shifted fair. Another day o' that storm an' we'd still have been beating up the Channel. I can tell you now you gave me quite a scare. How about coming aboard for dinner tomorrow? I've got a Chinese steward that cooks like a yellow angel."

Tea was a commodity that required quick handling. Sometimes its flavor was spoiled even in a fast ship if she had a wet voyage and her ventilation below decks was bad.

For that reason nobody aboard the *Javelin* was allowed shore leave until the last chest had been swung out of the hold. An agent of the company to which the tea had been consigned stood by to supervise the unloading. His report was complimentary. All the cargo had come through in good condition.

It was May 16 when Bob was able to get a day off. He went ashore in company with George Preble and Matt— the same little group that had explored the California gold fields. This was a very different expedition. The only thing that reminded Bob of San Francisco was the long squalid water front, with its grogshops and drunken sailormen. The Limehouse district teemed with the offscourings of many nations—Lascars and Chinese coolies, Greeks and Levantines and Portuguese.

Preble had been ashore in London once before. He steered his two young friends through the narrow streets till they had left the warehouses behind and could board a horse-drawn omnibus that took them westward. Around them the greatest city in the world began to unfold. They stared at such famous landmarks as London Bridge, the Houses of Parliament, Westminster Abbey, and St. Paul's. They lunched at an ancient chophouse off Piccadilly Circus, wandered through Hyde Park, and saw the tall, resplendent guards marching stiffly to and fro in front of Buckingham Palace.

By late afternoon they were standing on the Thames Embankment, watching the sunset shining on the river and glinting on the great dome of St. Paul's Cathedral. Below them, hundreds of small boats were moored along the waterside.

"Let's go back to the ship that way," Matt suggested. "Those boats are for hire, aren't they?"

"Sure," said Preble. "Good idea."

They descended the stone stairs and were greeted by a

villainous-looking Cockney who might have been the twin brother of Scully, the mutineer Bob had shot on the beach. Even the high, whiny voice was the same.

"Right 'ere, gents," said the waterman. "Tyke ye upstream or dahn—any plyce yer'd like to go."

"London Docks," Preble replied. "Ship *Javelin*. How much?"

The boatman's little rat eyes looked them over greedily. "Hamericans, eh," he said, licking his lips. "Arf a crown's the ryte—for each, that is."

They had money in their pockets and to Bob, at least, the fare sounded cheap enough. But Preble laughed and made as if to turn away. "We're no greenhorns," he said. "Three shillings for the lot would be more'n the trip's worth."

They finally settled for a crown—five shillings—and took their places in the wherry. For all his haggling, the boatman was an expert at his business. He sent the light craft darting down the river at surprising speed, dodging in and out among the other boats and barges and yelling curses at any who got in his way. In less than an hour they were back aboard the clipper.

"Get your fill of London?" Bill Wyatt asked as he greeted them. "It's probably your last chance this voyage. Something tells me the skipper'll be ready to sail again in a day or two. Then we'll really be homeward-bound!"

XIX

Nearly a third of the crew failed to answer roll call next morning. One or two were too badly hung-over to stand on their feet. The rest had either jumped ship or were sleeping off their binge in some water-front dive. The captain sent Red Gilman and a couple of dependable men ashore to try to round them up.

"Pick up anybody you see who looks like a seaman," he told the searchers. "I'd like to sail for Boston twenty-four hours from now."

Meanwhile, Sprague had Wing Lee pressing his best blue uniform. He had been invited, along with Captain Douglas of the *Western Star*, to a testimonial dinner given by the Tea Merchants' Association at the famous Ship and Turtle Tavern in Leadenhall Street.

He went ashore at six, and by nine-thirty that evening he was back aboard, rosy and merry after the festivities. Immediately he called the junior officers together.

"What's the report on the crew?" he asked.

"The bosun managed to pick up four," Wyatt told him. "Two of 'em were ours, an' both the others look like good able hands. One's a Salem man who wanted to get home. That leaves us only about seven short o' what we started with."

"I reckon that'll be enough to handle her," said the captain. "We don't have to crowd sail on this voyage home. Get her ready to cast off at high tide tomorrow morning."

All through the period while the cargo was being unloaded, the ship's carpenter and the sailmaker had been working at their jobs. Chips had repaired such damage as the ship had suffered in the storm off the Cape of Good Hope, and Sails had labored with his needle and palm, readying a new heavy-weather fore-topsail.

As soon as the watches were told off next morning, the crew was set to painting. They put in several hours of work before the tide turned, and continued while the ship was being towed down the Thames. About four o'clock in the afternoon paintpots and brushes were stowed and the hands were sent aloft to make sail.

The weather was bright and clear, but the breeze blew from the south. As soon as the clipper rounded the North Foreland, she had to start tacking, first far over toward the French coast, then back again till she was in sight of Deal and Dover. Through the night she kept it up, the men straining at the braces. Morning found her in mid-Channel, off Dungeness, and from that point on it was easier. They could make a long reach to the westward now, with the breeze abeam all the way to Land's End. But just as they passed the Lizard, late on the second day, there came a shift in the wind. Big swells rolled in from the open sea to meet the ship head-on, and Bob realized they had entered the booming westerlies.

On the quarterdeck, Captain Sprague ordered the course changed to southwest by south. A sailing ship, westbound across the Atlantic, had to take an indirect route unless she wanted to make a beat of it all the way. By cruising south till she was out of the westerlies, she could hope to pick up the northeast trades somewhere between the Azores and the Madeiras. Also, she could avoid the icebergs, which drifted down from Greenland at this time of year to make the northern route hazardous.

For two days they sailed across the Bay of Biscay, battling

rain and shifting winds. Then the weather cleared somewhere off Cape Finisterre, and they continued southwestward with a light breeze on the starboard beam. Six days out of London, at latitude 36° North, they caught the first breath of the trades. The yards were hauled around, the wind strengthened from the northeast, and the *Javelin* drove merrily westward under full sail.

From that point on, the crossing was all that a sailor could ask. Released from the need for work aloft and at the braces, all hands were set to swabbing decks, polishing brass, and touching up paint. The clipper's bottom was probably foul, after voyaging nearly around the world, but above the water line she had to look taut and shining, as befitted the fastest ship of the year.

On the third of June they were just northward of Bermuda and only seven hundred miles from the nearest American port. But Boston was their destination. Studying the charts, Bob felt a thrill of delight when Captain Sprague altered the course to north-northwest. Home lay that way, and soon they would have the added push of the Gulf Stream to hurry them on.

Heeled far to port, the ship plunged forward like a high-mettled horse that knew he was headed for the home barn. They logged three hundred miles that day, and their position at noon on June 6 was only a hundred miles southeast of Nantucket.

Bob and Matt Ryder grinned at each other. "If the wind holds," said Bob, "we ought to be in sight of Eastern Point by sunrise."

Bob had the early morning watch, from four to eight, and they were halfway across Cape Cod Bay when the sky began to lighten in the east. Bill Wyatt ordered the hands aloft to shorten sail. And just as the sun broke out of the sea astern, a pilot boat came scudding out of Boston Harbor to meet them. The *Javelin* was tied up in her old berth by nine o'clock that morning—June 7th, 1855.

* * *

Fourth Mate Wingate waited impatiently in the great, smoky barn of the Eastern Railroad Station. He had money in his pocket, a rail ticket, and a consuming eagerness to get home. The three days he had spent in Boston had been busy and interesting enough, but what he really wanted was to reach the comfortable old house between the blue water and the green hills of Kittery. The one train that ran to Portsmouth each day was scheduled to leave at ten o'clock.

There had been a fine reunion with Matt Ryder's parents at the wharfside. Bob had dined at their house that evening, and the next day he had gone ashore alone to make some purchases. Boston no longer awed him as it had on his first visit. Handsome as the old city was, it seemed small compared to the teeming congestion of Canton or the vastness and dignity of London.

He went to two or three of the best shops. For his mother he bought a beautiful silk shawl and a length of flowered dress goods. A suitable gift for his father took more thought. Finally he remembered the battered old nickel-cased watch that Tobias Wingate had carried for years, and he chose a good silver one with a Swiss movement. In addition, he had his gold nugget mounted on a stickpin for his father's tie.

These things were carefully packed in his seabag now. Wing Lee had cleaned and pressed his brass-buttoned blue uniform, and he had on a new white officer's cap with a black brim and band. Unconsciously he held himself straighter in all this finery. He had grown an inch or two during the voyage, and his lean, sun-browned face had a stern look that made him appear older than his seventeen years.

Before he left the ship, Captain Sprague had taken him into the cabin for a few words in private.

"You've done mighty well, boy," he said. "I was right when I thought you had the makings of a sailor and an officer. Here's your pay and you've earned it. The owners are happy over this voyage, as they should be. What with the profit on the cargo we took to California and the sixty-odd thousand dollars we earned carrying tea, the *Javelin*'s paid for herself already. I turned over the owners' half of what we made from the furs, and after giving a good big purse to Langdon's widow, there's still some left. Your share's a thousand dollars. Maybe that'll help convince your father he was right to let you go."

He smiled and shook Bob's hand. "We'll be sailing again in about two months—three at the outside. Have to get the ship's bottom cleaned first. I've got your address and I'll let you know a week or two before you're needed. Your mate's berth, by the way, is permanent."

At last the puffing little wood-burning locomotive, with its great stack, was backed into the station and coupled to the three cars. Bob chose a seat in the forward car next to a right-hand window. And when all the passengers were aboard, the train chugged out across the river on its northward way.

Once they were out in the country, the June morning seemed to be full of warmth and sunshine. All along the right of way there were farmers in their hayfields, swinging scythes. The noise of the engine drowned out the songs of the bobolinks, but the boy could see the little black-and-white birds flying high above the ripe clover.

He wondered, as he had many times, how things were going at home. For nine months now he had been com-

pletely cut off from his parents, though he had written them
once from San Francisco and again from London. The
train, chuffing smokily along at twenty miles an hour,
seemed terribly slow.

It was past noon when they crossed the Merrimac at New-
buryport. A man came through the cars selling sandwiches,
doughnuts, and coffee, but Bob wasn't hungry. He watched
eagerly for glimpses of the sea as the train labored on
through the Hamptons. This was New Hampshire now,
and Portsmouth was only a dozen miles away. The air was
clear. Once, when the tracks ran close to the shore, he
looked across the water and caught sight of a bit of land on
the far horizon—the Isles of Shoals.

"Portsmouth!" shouted the conductor at last. "All out
for Portsmouth! An' don't leave any packages in the cars."

The train slowed and finally jerked to a clanking stop.
Bob was already up and pushing toward the door. With his
seabag on his shoulder, he went down the steps and looked
along the platform, but there was nobody there he knew.

Most of the passengers were being greeted by friends or relatives. He wished, now, that he had written home the day he made port and asked his father to meet him. Instead he had decided to surprise his family. But it made him feel lonesome to be the only stranger in the crowd.

Walking with long strides through the streets, he made his way down toward the ferry landing. Ahead of him he saw a broad-shouldered figure that looked familiar. As he drew abreast, he recognized Abijah Lowe, the foreman of the Rogers and Hale shipyard.

"Well, if it ain't young Wingate!" said Lowe. "Ye ain't been 'round to see us much lately. Been away?"

The friendly but casual greeting took some of Bob's conceit out of him. He laughed and nodded. "I shipped out aboard the *Javelin*," he said. "Remember when you launched her, 'most a year ago? I've been clear 'round the world since I saw you last. What's the word over in Kittery? Ma an' Dad all right?"

"They was to church last Sunday, an' both lookin' fine. Don't they know ye're home?"

"No," Bob admitted. "I meant to surprise 'em. You got any new clippers on the ways?"

"Only one. She's the *Noonday*, for Hastings o' Boston. Be ready to launch in about a month, I reckon. Say—didn't I hear the *Javelin* had broke the Californy record or somethin'?"

"Not quite. Came almighty close, though. Well, I'll be home for a spell, so I'll be seeing you."

He had luck at the ferry slip, for the boat had just come in. Hurrying forward to the bow, he set down his duffel and drew a deep breath of the breeze off the Narrows. Its flavor was different from that of the deep sea. It smelled of fish and lobsters, of tide flats and kelpy rocks—a rich, homelike smell that he had missed more than he knew.

Three or four buggies and farm wagons clattered aboard,

187

the gates were shut, the whistle tooted, and the paddles began to churn. The tide was coming in and the ferryboat had to claw her way, crab-fashion, to the other side. That meant the crossing took a few minutes longer. But at last the blunt bow nosed into the Kittery slip.

It was past two o'clock now and the noonday meal was long since over, yet the boy could have sworn he smelled clam chowder cooking. His step quickened as he strode along up the sandy road. There, under the big horse-chestnut tree, was the house. He saw that it had a fresh coat of white paint, and the roof had been patched with a sprinkling of new, light-colored shingles. In the yard was the old dory in which his mother grew her geraniums and petunias. Bees hummed drowsily around the flowers and the summer afternoon was full of peace.

He set his bag down on the porch and knocked gently at the door. After the second knock his mother called from upstairs.

"Who's there?"

"A sailor," he answered. "Just a sailor, home from a voyage."

He heard the patter of her feet as she flew down the stairs, and then they were in each other's arms. Her eyes were wet with happy tears when she finally pulled away to look up at him.

"Bob," she panted, "that's an officer's uniform!"

"That's right," he told her. "Fourth mate. How's Dad?"

"Never better. And you look wonderful—only you're too thin. Probably haven't had a bite of dinner!"

He laughed. "Ma," he said, "I didn't know it till this minute, but I'm starved. Don't suppose you've got anything left over, have you?"

"Chowder," she replied. "Half a kettle of it, still hot. And I'll warm up the biscuits to eat with beach plum preserve. And there's some apple pie. Think that'll hold you till suppertime?"

She bustled off to the kitchen, and he laughed again and stretched his arms. "Now," he called to her, "I know I'm really home!"